Ferdinand

❦

the Man
with the
Kind Heart

OTHER PRESS

NEW YORK

Ferdinand

the Man
with the
Kind Heart

IRMGARD KEUN

Translated from the German
by Michael Hofmann

Original title: *Ferdinand, der Mann*
mit dem freundlichen Herzen
© by Ullstein Buchverlage GmbH, Berlin.
Published in 2019 by Ullstein Taschenbuch Verlag
and 1981 by Claassen Verlag. First published in 1950.

Translation copyright © 2020 Other Press

The translation of this work was supported by a grant
from the Goethe-Institut.

Production editor: Yvonne E. Cárdenas
Text designer: Jennifer Daddio
This book was set in Filosofia by
Alpha Design & Composition of Pittsfield, NH

1 3 5 7 9 10 8 6 4 2

Library of Congress Cataloging-in-Publication Data

Names: Keun, Irmgard, 1905-1982, author. | Hofmann,
    Michael, 1957 August 25- translator.
Title: Ferdinand, the man with the kind heart /
    Irmgard Keun ; translated from the German
    by Michael Hofmann.
Other titles: Ferdinand, der Mann mit dem
    freundlichen Herzen. English
Description: New York : Other Press, [2020] | Original
    title: Ferdinand, der Mann mit dem freundlichen
    Herzen; © by Ullstein Buchverlage GmbH, Berlin.
Published in 2019 by Ullstein Taschenbuch Verlag and
    1981 by Claassen Verlag. First published in 1950.
    Identifiers: LCCN 2020027851 (print) |
    LCCN 2020027852 (ebook) | ISBN 9781635420357
    (paperback) | ISBN 9781635420364 (ebook)
    Classification: LCC PT2621.E92 F4713 2020 (print) |
    LCC PT2621.E92 (ebook) | DDC 833/.912—dc23
    LC record available at https://lccn.loc.gov/2020027851
    LC ebook record available at https://lccn.loc.
        gov/2020027852

Translator's Note

Anyone who has read her other books (*Gilgi, One of Us*; *The Artificial Silk Girl*; *After Midnight*; and *Child of All Nations*) will know Irmgard Keun (1905–82) to be an original: a witty, fearless, and unpredictable writer of the Weimar and exile periods. The last novel she published, *Ferdinand, the Man with the Kind Heart*, is a book from a unique circumstance, an underlit time, and an important place: 1950, the year after the division of Germany (until then under the jurisdiction of the four Allied powers, Russia, France, Britain, and the United States) was made official and permanent, with the proclamation of the two rival nations of West and East Germany (the former Russian sector). As Keun puts it, with her typical, unmistakeable dryness, "Our former unlamented German dictatorship has, in the way of lower life-forms, procreated by simple fission, and is now called democracy." Imagine a novel about the very early days of the *Wirtschaftswunder* by the wise cynic and author of *Candide*, Voltaire, and you have *Ferdinand, the Man with the Kind Heart*.

Ferdinand is a book where things have been codified or heralded or announced—the rival republics, the oft-invoked currency reform, the beginnings of prosperity—but are yet to happen properly. It is a book of ironic healing, false growth, and improvised hopes; where a stupidly contrived tabloid unreality offers distraction to the plenty seeking it ("Man seeks divorce after wife abandons him in bowl of unsalted spinach"); a cocktail of fear and avidity and nosiness and absurdity; of "New Look," and repurposed coats, and kerchiefs for hats, and where the whole idea of genders and hierarchies and careers and households is yet to be re-established. Where all the characters—and the author too, one might guess—were chancers, running around in a state of shock lit by flashbacks and addled by official optimism. "He informed me that he had changed horses and was now a law student." Conditions are still soft, mutable, adaptive, evolving. A social-Darwinian moment for the upwardly mobile fish to acquire legs. The endearingly slow Ferdinand, getting his marching orders, is apologetically rejected as "a man for abnormal times."

But full legality, normality, remain a ways off. Production and consumption are both in their infancy. No one here follows a useful or a respectable calling. The atmosphere remains conditioned by crime and the memory of crime: "Insatiable and obsessed, my forget-me-not-blue mother-in-law went on the prowl, and snaffled among other things a sewing machine, various typewriters, four rugs, seventeen eggcups, a gilt frame, a bombproof door, a poultry cage, and a pompous drawing-room painting depicting a voluptuous woman lying prone in pink, puffy nudity, a blue moth teetering on the end of her pink index finger, and the whole thing somehow casual." No one in this book lives in a house, has a regular family, a job, a budget, a plan. (Or else they have too many plans.) They are urgent and primitive in their biological needs, which are principally for terrible drink, even worse cigarettes, and one another. Where the Victorian novel aspires to stability and marriage, *Ferdinand* deals in the provisional, in pashes and penury. It is an anti-romance (our hero finally succeeds in shaking off his fiancée, and lands up in his sleeping mother's hotel bedroom, with her alert dachshund and two whimsically adopted black children, referred to as Negroes, but that was the style of the fifties, and there's not the least malice in Keun, never mind anything like racist feeling) and an anti-*Entwicklungsroman* (he ends, our unhappy veteran of war and peace, having learned little or nothing, if anything rather behind where he began). "I feel so deep-frozen," he muses, and we with him, "I wonder if I'll ever thaw out in this life." The moment it is all set in, though, is precious and fleeting, the cultural equivalent of the predawn evoked in the words of Ferdinand's cousin Johanna, the great free spirit of the book. "Look at that, Ferdinand—see the sky on fire! It's the sunrise. In an hour's time the first bailiff will be here."

—M. H.

Ferdinand

✶

the Man
with the
Kind Heart

I have an article to write

.
.
.

❦

.
.
.

I am puzzled each time anyone supposes I have money. It began with the pickpocket. The most recent instance was Heinrich, who couldn't believe I wanted an advance for the article he wanted me to write.

I have never written an article in my life, but Heinrich was insistent, and I don't like to say no. For the past week, Heinrich has been the editor of an apolitical weekly paper called *Red Dawn*, and he is a mild and blameless person.

With my fifty marks, I bought a pack of Belgian cigarettes and a bottle of Moselle and settled down in my room to compose. Frau Stabhorn, my landlady, supported my efforts with a stub of pencil and the tattered exercise book of one of her grandchildren. Now the paper is willing, but the spirit is weak. What on earth am I going to write?

The Moselle tastes as flaccid and murky as the decayed philanthropy of an unhappily married vintner. The Belgian cigarettes taste of rancid hay. I wasn't in Belgium during the war and have never harmed a hair on the head of any Belgian. In the event that these Belgian cigarettes don't constitute collective punishment but some individual act of revenge, then it seems to me this is another case of the wrong person catching it. A grey melancholy lames my mind. And there I was, promising myself stimulation through the use of . . . stimulants.

My room at Frau Stabhorn's—Emmy Stabhorn, née Baske, widow—isn't a proper room at all, but the passageway between her kitchen–living room and her bedroom. It has the feeling of a stretch coffin. The kitchen door was purloined during the last month of the war by the neighbor, Lydia Krake, and chopped up for firewood. Said Lydia straightaway came under suspicion, and this was duly confirmed by the one-eyed seer on Engelbertstrasse. In spite of which Lydia Krake and Frau Stabhorn remained on-again, off-again besties.

Prior to the currency reform,[*] they were both engaged in diverse black-market schemes, which they pursued with the nervous tenacity that imparts the fiery gleam of sexual sunset to the financial machinations of aging ladies.

Lydia Krake was the occasional supplier of fresh meat whose provenance remained, at least as far as I was concerned, obscure and unexplained. I was trusted, but never let into the secret. To be more precise, I wasn't taken seriously.

Because I was hungry, I was offered some of the meat. Probably it was so that they might see how its consumption would affect the human organism. Acts of impulsive charity were not in the nature of Frau Krake or Frau Stabhorn. The meat perked me up and seemed to do me no harm. It wasn't a varietal I had previously encountered. Perhaps it came from exotic animals that had perished in one of the zoos. I only hope it wasn't

---

[*] Of 20 and 21 June 1948.

human. Eating human flesh carries adverse long-term consequences.

The one-eyed seer was also involved in the trade, till one day found him in ugly opposition to the ladies. To their profound satisfaction he had to go to prison later for falsification of ration cards. On the day of his arrest, his two antagonists were all sweetness and light. They laid cards for each other, a wistful return to the habits of their fortune-telling mothers. Shortly afterwards, though, they were once more sundered, this time over a mild-mannered theology-student-cum-spiv, to whom Frau Stabhorn had given a hundred elastic corsets on commission. Lydia Krake had sunk some of her precious capital in the corsets. The theology student vanished without trace. God knows what he did with the corsets. Not long ago I ran into him outside a stall that sold potato pancakes. He informed me that he had changed horses and was now a law student.

The little Stabhorns stream into the kitchen through the door that isn't a door. They like to swing on the sticky curtain that separates my room from their grandmother's bedroom. At night, I hear Frau Stabhorn snoring. By day, the curtain gives way every two or three hours. It is among my tasks to reattach it.

The ceiling of my room is all holes. The house suffers from age and natural decay. It's like a gouty pensioner, who has no more reason to shave or smell nice.

Even in its youth, it won't have had much in the way of charm. No traces persist of onetime beauty—not like the old ladies in fin de siècle novels. What it does bear are traces of bomb damage.

I have tried several times to plaster over the holes in the ceiling. Probably the plaster is no good, because it keeps falling out—to the delight of the children, who use it to mark hopscotch boxes on the floor.

The Stabhorn family consists of Frau Stabhorn and numerous grandchildren. From time to time various daughters and sons-in-law appear, to greet the existing children with noisy affection and drop off another one. The Stabhorn breed is vigorous and prolific.

I know that a dislike of children exposes one to the horrified contempt of all political parties and the main religious and atheistical philosophies. Children are the bonny little blossoms in the moldering garden of life. As I write, a couple of the bonny little blossoms are trying to spread a mixture of jam and plaster of paris all over my arms and legs.

Among other things, Frau Stabhorn dealt in illicit jam. One of her sons-in-law seems to be sitting on the source of an inexhaustible supply of it. There are buckets of it all over, the whole flat is sticky with it. After the currency reform, the flood of jam dried up for a while. Jammy traces on furniture and infants started to congeal and lost some of their stickiness. But now things are

as they were. Jam everywhere. A sweet, red, toxic jam.
A decidedly malignant jam, the enjoyment of which is
followed by repentance.

If it looked anything like it tasted, the jam would have
to be green—a lurid poison green like absinthe, or maybe
turquoise with a contrary touch of purple, like the nightmare vision of one of those degenerate painters.

You're prepared to eat many things if you're hungry,
but I think for myself that if this jam were green instead
of red I wouldn't be able to get it down. Though, actually,
why not? What's wrong with a blue tomato? Or a lemon-
yellow veal chop? Isn't it all acculturation and biological
conservatism? I wonder how many more prejudices I'd
find myself guilty of if I thought seriously?

At this point, I could write either a forensic disqui-
sition or a surrealist elegy on jam. But I think Heinrich
would say his readers weren't interested in anything so
depressing. Or I'd have to turn the jam story into something incomprehensible, like late Hölderlin or early
Rilke. The incomprehensible always gets a free pass
from the reader. He imagines he understands it, and that
makes him feel good about himself.

Every now and again Frau Stabhorn comes skipping through my room. Her semilegal existence hasn't
worn her down; on the contrary it's kept her vitally
trim. Sometimes I think hateful thoughts and wish that
instead of giving her grandchildren jam to play with

she would give them a hearty spanking. But she's not a spanker. She's chirrupy and excited and she skips. Earlier she used to skip around my bed. Not from any carnal motive, but because she kept her stock of black-market cigarettes under my mattress. I don't know what about the Widow Stabhorn might be enviable aside from her cheerfulness, but I know her to be widely envied. Envious neighbors, so she claims anyway, denounce her to the police. Then I have to lie in bed and play the poor, invalid returnee. The Widow Stabhorn would shed compassionate tears when she told the policeman about me. My bed has never been searched for contraband or substandard goods. It has been known for policemen to offer me cigarettes from the supply with which they had just been bribed.

I suppose I could write about my bed. At the head and foot it has bars of lamentable metal. I wonder who came up with that idea, and why? Why the waste of metal? If the bars were at the sides, that would at least have the effect of preventing a sufferer from nightmares from falling out. But show me the person who ever fell out of bed via the head end or the foot end. So why the bars? As an ornament? Who would take an imitation of prison bars for ornamentation? So, no, I don't want to write about that. I'm sure readers would have zero interest in an account of prison bars, broken springs, and the damaged psychology of bed manufacturers.

Why do I have to write something anyway?

It all began with the pickpocket. I was standing outside the opera, waiting for the tram to take me to my cousin Johanna.

The November day was as grey as a whole wagon-load of Prayer and Repentance days.[*] May God forgive me, but I have something against Prayer and Repentance Day. It offends my democratic sense of freedom to be told to repent by some external authority that has no business in my inner life. Given our terrible climate, November is wall-to-wall expiation anyway. Everything ought to be done to cheer people up this month. Fountains of red wine should spring up on street corners, airplanes should scatter flowering lilac boughs from the skies, bands of jolly musicians should process through the town. Municipal, tax, and post offices should be decked out with red lights, public officials should wear parrot feathers and garlands, and prosecutors and judges should punctuate legal proceedings with nifty little dances. Heads of state, finance ministers, and the like should be kept from giving speeches or from taking a position on any of the important matters of the day—at best, they might be allowed to run a carousel for the free use of disadvantaged youngsters.

---

[*] German Buss-und-Bettag, November 4., a Lutheran celebration (Cologne is very largely Catholic).

Such a profligate mode of life would require the approval of the relevant ministries. But November and fog and grey and morality and repentance—that's too much. It gnaws at the marrow of the hardworking citizen, it saps the will to live, it's enough to lay low the most resistant elector.

So I was standing at the tram stop in the grey mizzle thinking all kinds of colorful thoughts in an effort to animate my inner landscape. A damp chill was making its way up through my leaky soles.

When the tram arrived, there was a sudden crush, as though they were handing out thousand-mark notes inside. The people surged forward as though it was a matter of getting to their loved-one's deathbed or on board the last aerial lifeboat to Mars.

I find it hard to believe that these grim elbowers and pushers were only trying to get home. Or to work. Or to some task or other. Their elbows were pointed, their muscles taut, their lips compressed with resolve. The look in their eyes became steely and hard. Ancient crones fought for a place in the sun with muscular factory workers, with pallidly resolute clerks, with grimly furious housewives. Children wailed, dragged into close-quarters combat by their berserk mothers. Satchel-toting youths insinuated themselves into the crush—their flailing technique gave them a great advantage. They pressed past everyone except one single old lady. She would not give way, would not step aside, she rammed her shopping bag full of earthy carrots into the hair and faces of the oncomers. She stood up on the running board, holding the balustrade with her free hand, her felt hat was skew-whiff—she pushed on, she had captured the platform, she was within sniffing distance of the conductor's armpit. She had won! She looked wildly about her, panting. Perhaps she was in training for the next Olympics.

The justification for such lethal barging, at least for any rational being, could only be paradise. Inasmuch as one can imagine any sort of paradise on earth. I think of it differently every day. Today my vision is of a mild bed of clouds in smiling light, in blue sky. Somewhere there are orange balls and velvety silver leaves and dark green. A pink flamingo flies with the pinions an old eagle has developed in wise solitude, singing with the gentleness of a newly opened cowslip on the forest edge. Like a nightingale.

It occurs to me I have never heard a nightingale. The nightingale is the most important bird in literature. No mediocre poem without its nightingale, no good poem either. The nightingale sobs, the nightingale cries, the nightingale toots and whistles. For hundreds of years, poets have been dining off nightingales. I have read and heard so much about nightingales, I really believed I knew nightingales . And I have never heard a nightingale. That shows you how well publicity works, and I always thought I would never fall for publicity. Do night-ingales even exist?

You never know if you'll live to see another day. If I'm spared till next summer, then I'll go and listen to a nightingale. I hope I don't forget. There's so much you forget to do or neglect to do. I wonder if any of the poets who wrote and sang about nightingales ever with their own ears heard a nightingale?

But nightingales here or there, I don't want to write my piece about them, even though the daily press likes it when authors write about a thing of which they have no knowledge. Profound ignorance persuades great cir-cles of readers; others find it sympathetic. Never mind the critical remnant, they feel strengthened in their self-confidence, confirmed in their superiority, and empowered in their protests, which keep their intel-lectual muscle from dwindling away. I assume too that the subject of nightingales has been green-lighted and would not be censored by the greater part of our current German dictatorships. For reasons of morality, a lot of things are censored today. Dictatorships are always very strict about what they understand as morals and public ethics. Our former unlamented German dictatorship has, in the way of lower life-forms, procreated by simple fission, and is now called democracy.

At the tram stop, I refrain from barging. I have oodles of time, and what one has, one ought to enjoy mindfully. As I stood there, mindfully, I suddenly felt a hand scrabbling about in my pocket. I reached for the hand and gripped it firmly by the wrist. A man in his middle years had been attempting to rob me. Poor fellow. All I had was a multiple ticket with one ride left on it, and that was in my other pocket. "Walk slowly, don't run, in your calling it's best to avoid drawing attention to oneself," I said to the man, and let go of his wrist. He ran like the clappers across Rudolfplatz. A beginner, I daresay, an amateur.

I felt flattered that the man had thought me worth robbing. You see, I wear neither hat nor coat, just a rather curious jerkin, with small natty skirts. It's sort of New Look, I tailored it myself from a lady's coat with history, back when I was released from the POW camp. My cousin Johanna likes to say I look like a hurdy-gurdy man's monkey when I'm wearing it. Hurdy-gurdy men's monkeys are sweet creatures, no doubt about it. I wouldn't mind looking a little more imposing, though.

While I was still enjoying the afterglow of the pickpocket, the tram departed, and I was thwacked on the back in a powerful and populist manner. It was my cousin Magnesius, who is a notorious thwacker of backs. "Come and have a beer with me," he said, and we disappeared into the nearest hostelry.

I was surprised at his generosity. He is accommodating, but usually only to himself. He is a man in pomp and pink. People who endure a meatless diet must be tempted to bite him in the cheek. I'm not quite sure how I came to be related to him. I'm related to so many people, I have relatives all over the world. All my various parents and grandparents scattered offspring all over the world, the way the Crown Prince scatters confetti. I even have some relatives who have money, but they tend to avoid me like the plague. Poverty is not just a disgrace, it's the only disgrace. If I were a millionaire, I could quite happily have done time without losing an iota of my social standing.

"You shouldn't have let him run off like that," said Magnesius. He had observed the incident with the pickpocket.

Dear Lord, why wouldn't I let the man run off? Ever since I could think, there have been people all over the world busily trying to destroy me. They come up with wars for me, and financial and political disasters. Small bombs, big bombs, atom bombs, super-atom bombs, death rays, poison gas, and all sorts of other vilenesses. All for me. And I'm to find a self-respecting pickpocket dangerous and noxious? At most, I might feel guilty about disappointing him.

Magnesius finds this to be a dubious morality.

"You must think about the generality, Ferdinand, the well-being of the generality." He raises a pudgy finger. "Where would we be if everyone thought like you!"

Where would Magnesius be? is what he means.
When he talks about the generality, he means himself. He's a nice man and all things to himself. He
goes around, and he comes around. When I got out of
prisoner-of-war camp, I went looking for him. Maybe
he could have got me a job as a driver or an office worker.
I'm not ambitious, and well suited to inferior work. But
Magnesius would have nothing to do with me. He sees
impoverished relatives as an acute danger to himself. He
gives nothing to charity, on principle. I'm sure he's right.
If rich people were openhanded, they wouldn't be rich.

I think Magnesius is currently something in non-
ferrous metals. "Well, cheers, Magnesius, your health."

He wasn't in the forces, and thinks of himself as a
pacifist, anti-militarist, and martyr—just right for now.
He is proud of the cunning he showed during the war to
avoid being called up. Magnesius is one of those heavy-
hipped individuals who lead a charmed life. No bombs
fall where they happen to be. The ships they sail on don't
sink. The trains in which they travel aren't derailed—or
at least their personal carriage stays intact. Popular
opinion conforms to them and their requirements. They
always have money, and they always have enough to eat.

Magnesius is not smart. My cousin Johanna even
thinks he is stupid. "Oh, Ferdinand," she says, "I don't
understand it. He's no more clever than a politician
or a bunny rabbit, but in five wars' time he will be

synthesizing vegetable oil and ham out of bomb craters. He won't be drinking potato vodka but French liqueurs, even when Europe has ceased to exist. After the hundred thousandth currency reform, he'll still find himself with freshly minted money. He will do deals with ghosts when there are no more people, he will..."

Sure he will. Just because of not being smart. Rabbits aren't smart either, but they can find what they need by way of fodder. Better than any Kant, Copernicus, Mozart, or Rembrandt.

Cheers, Magnesius! One day he'll have a stroke, a mild, gentle one, and then he'll talk God or the Devil into some material spun from nothing but hanging beautifully, especially good for hard-wearing, flowing robes, or he'll sell Sirius a bale of antiqued blackout paper. He will live, and live well, even when he's dead.

Shall I write my story about Magnesius? Better not. Germany is supposed to be being refashioned into a democracy. When did any amount of fashioning bring about the wished-for result? The world is ajangle with weaponry, the core of the planet is a gleaming uniform button, laboratories are now super-arsenals, but the order of the day is of course anti-militarism. Why and what for? Any general is like a sweet and harmless Parma violet by comparison to an industrial chemist. And Magnesius? The implacably opposed to war? The unrequitably in love with war? Who harvests where life has scattered no seeds, and death has reaped? I know soldiers, both old and young, who hated the war as much as the voice of their sergeant majors and loved peace like the lips of their bride. Who had more familiarity with lockup than stonk. By his existence or the mere account of it, Magnesius could make militarists of them all.

Magnesius ordered a second bottle of wine and talked to me as though to an equal. About financial crises, bank credits, bankruptcies, crooked deals, lowered business ethics. I listened to him shakenly and respectfully. What on earth was the matter with him? He had never been like that before. Not long ago, I read about brain operations that were supposed to change a person's entire personality. Or had Magnesius perhaps come within reach of some radioactive rays? Or had a magic quack treated his blood pressure and attained these unexpected results?

"Cheers, Ferdinand. You know, you really ought to invest your money in something, my boy, I could help you do it." I failed to understand Magnesius. "You ought to get yourself a new suit." Did he want to buy me one, then? "Yes, and those hundred marks I lent you, no hurry about paying them back, Ferdinand."

I guessed there was some misunderstanding. Before I made an attempt to clear it up, I let Magnesius order a round of deviled eggs. Cautiously, I tried to wrap my head around whatever might concern me.

I heard some ugly things about Johanna. My cousin Johanna is ravishing but unscrupulous. Not long ago, she bet that she could get a hundred marks out of Magnesius. I bet her five marks she couldn't. Johanna told Magnesius I had won thirteen hundred marks on the pools and was looking to invest the money with him. Would he let her have a hundred marks for me. Johanna is a convincing liar. I wonder when I'll lay my hands on the five marks I owe her.

I was too cowardly to make a clean breast of things to Magnesius. He is one of those people who go blue when they're furious. I don't like to see that.

I acted distrait, shamefaced, nervous. I made an appointment to see Magnesius sometime next week, and said I needed to be alone. I wanted to think about financial matters.

Magnesius went, and in came Heinrich. He stood in front of my table, whose fair wood I wanted to go on enjoying a little, quietly, by myself. There was something warmer and kindlier than the dank November streets, and my coffin room at the Widow Stabhorn's.

"Oh, Ferdinand," said Heinrich, and "you don't mind if I call you by your first name, do you? Can I join you?" Of course he could. He was nice and neat, as though bespoke. He had a wily face and trusty border collie's eyes. I barely knew him, but why shouldn't he call me by my first name?

"So you're still alive!" I exclaimed delightedly. It's impossible for me to say to a person who greets me thus, "Terribly sorry, I haven't the foggiest idea who you are."

Heinrich sat down and ordered a bottle of wine. "Do you remember?" he asked, "that wild night in Berlin in wartime, when we drank brotherhood? You liked it that my name was Heinrich." I didn't, but I was happy at least to learn the name of my brand-new friend.

"A votre santé," said Heinrich, cultured and well-bred, and raised his glass. "You know, I have always admired you, Ferdinand."

I was stunned. I never guessed there was a living being that had always admired me. What a day! The pickpocket, Magnesius, and now Heinrich. Three people, showing me their high opinion of me. And the day not over yet.

Heinrich is the editor of *Red Dawn*. It started coming out a week ago, or is due to appear next week, I'm a little shaky about that. I think for the moment they have no paper, no license, and no contributions, apart from an anecdote about Caruso. Heinrich said it was difficult to suit all readers, you were bound to antagonize someone. We agree to meet later that evening. In the meantime, I am to write an unexceptionable story.

What actually does appear in our popular postwar periodicals? I can't formulate a single impression, because thus far my reading has been confined to the little squares of newsprint that are hung out in lieu of toilet paper in the WC on the landing. These fragments have occasional charm, but in the long run they are a little superficial.

I sometimes got the impression that Germany was part of the British monarchy. Wall-to-wall court reports. Too bad Princess Elizabeth can't get married again. Then I would have a subject with which to delight great swaths of readers for months on end. I also came upon many reports and photographs of Princess Margaret. Could I write about her? I don't think she has much to offer. I had the sense of a nice girl from a good family. If reports are to be trusted, she spends her time dancing the boogie-woogie, buying clothes, traveling abroad, and climbing in and out of automobiles. Which is all about the least one can expect. Couldn't the little lady steal the crown jewels for me, or hide the Loch Ness monster in the House of Lords, elope with an archbishop, and re-main gone at least until I've made a thousand marks with my series of quietly nerve-tingling articles?

Or is there some film actress I could develop? I've read various interviews. The hack goes to meet the star. The star is photographed lying on a summer lawn, chewing on a blade of grass. It looks terribly natural. The star receives her visitor, makes coffee, hangs up her underthings—"See, I do this all myself"—stirs something in a saucepan, knits socks, prefers

Schopenhauer and lighter reading, repairs a carpet sweeper, is a believer in the economic miracle. The piece closes, "I left Anna Fischer with the sense that I had met an utterly natural person. 'Ma'am,' I said, 'you don't behave like a star.' 'Here comes my star,' she smiled, lifting her three-year-old into her arms. And now I must break it to the reader: Anna Fischer, whom we hopefully may admire many more times on the screen, is a happily married young mother, the wife of the noted architect Walter Leibund, who is known for his work in concrete and brick. Anna Fischer is no prima donna."

I should like, for a change, to write about prima donnas. But just at the moment the fashion is for the "natural" star with solid family background, and the dictatorship of the readership will permit no exceptions.

I think perhaps the least offense is caused by animal stories. I am fond of animals, though I don't enjoy being played off against them. Acquaintances of mine had a Doberman, a vicious creature that couldn't get its inner life in harmony with its surroundings. His master be-came a megalomaniac, because he was the only person the animal didn't growl at and bite. He bit me in the ear, and the fellow told me I had failed the test. A dog like that had an infallible sense of good and bad. It contra-dicts my sense of human dignity to be subjected to the judgment of a dog. There was one occasion when I denied myself further dealings with a well-disposed lady with mild eyes and a splendid bosom merely because her terrier was allergic to quiet conversations and set itself up to judge my spiritual qualities. I am prepared to lavish any amount of ingenious flattery on the lady of the house, but I don't like to feel obliged to come with orchids and volumes of verse for her dog.

So what is the animal I could write about? Hens? All I know about hens is that they lay eggs, their inner life is an enigma to me. I like giraffes, they have spots. But there's no story in that.

The animals I know best are probably cockroaches. I am well acquainted with their habits and preferences. I know that they don't bark, have a strong sense of community, don't talk about politics, and lead a respectable family life in the sense of calm and busy proliferation. Unfortunately, Heinrich is bound to think a gentleman should not display such knowledge of cockroaches.

How about a love story then? I will assume a man and a girl are in love, and will begin with a snatch of realistic dialogue.

"Do you love me, Darling?"

"Yes, I love you, Darling."

"Do you love me very much, Darling?"

"Yes, I love you very much, Darling—do you love me too, Darling?"

"But you know I do, Darling."

"Do you pine for me sometimes, Darling?"

"Would I be here otherwise, Darling?"

"Are you my darling?"

"Yes, I am your darling, Darling."

They say that a writer should constantly strive for the truth. This lovey-dovey dialogue is the complete truth, but from the literary point of view, it seems somewhat wanting. It's my sense that the more people are in love, the simpler and more unevolved their speech. Love will cause the most extensive vocabulary to melt away like snow under burning lava. I can remember myself having babbled like an idiot on occasion. I have no desire to document this and commit it to print for all time.

It's not so easy to write a love story in today's Germany. There are strict laws.

Extramarital love may only take place under certain defined conditions. Erotic displays are permitted only in conjunction with nature. For instance: the blonde Erdmute and her soulful swain Horst Dieter are riding through woods and fields. They are surprised by a thunderstorm. It starts hailing, lightning, snowing. The formula goes, "The elements were unchained." Erdmute and Horst Dieter take refuge in a barn that happens to be in the vicinity. The barn contains hay. It's dark as well. Horst Dieter presses Erdmute to himself. Everything collapses. The reader will forgive them, because storm, barn, and hay all constitute mitigating circumstances.

I know a thing or two about barns. They are unromantic and not at all exciting places. Rusty watering cans and pickaxes are liable to fall on top of you. Hay is a prickly and dusty substance that will make you sneeze. For a normal person, a love scene in a barn is not a pleasure. That is probably the reason why storm-barn-love scenes are literarily sanctioned. If it's no fun, it's less sinful. Also, the strong connection to nature will make the reader more inclined to forgive the odd faux pas. He may very well turn a blind eye when the tormented pair falls victim to a pine-needle-scented forest floor. A forest floor isn't exactly fun either. Ants crawl into your ears, pine needles prick at you, midges bite you. There is a bird singing in a tree and it happens to drop something. You must expect to be interrupted at any moment by forest wardens, hunters, tramps, lyric poets, and berry-seeking children. You can't shut the door in a forest. If a twig happens to crack somewhere, you jump. Maybe it's just a deer. But then I wouldn't want to have a deer listening as I'm pouring out my secret heart to the lady of my dreams. Call me overly modest. Perhaps my subconscious takes a deer for the reincarnation of an old nanny I once had. On top of everything, the light summer dress of the errant lady would suffer—thorns and dirt and the like. One would suppose that for a broad public a fall from grace is just that, a fall from grace, no matter where it happens to take place. Myself, I would accord any amorous couple a nice room with a couch or a paradise bed. But I don't think one is allowed to say that without it robbing the couple of all sympathies from the readership. In poems you are allowed to be more generous, and still more in poems that are set to music. My most straitlaced and prudish aunts got a misty look in their eyes and hummed along when a velvet tenor sang in the wireless, "Be mine tonight..." or "There's a small hotel I know / in the Wieden..." or "It's now or never..." All those things may be sung with impunity, but not said, and least of all printed. Why? I'll think about it sometime. At any rate, I don't trust myself to write a love story. I would have to punish my lovers terribly for their sins, which I'd sooner not do.

Perhaps I could tell the story of my little jerkin?

I was in the POW camp. For as long as I could remember, I'd been and done only what others wanted. I hardly knew whether I still existed as a self-determining living creature. In the war I was punished by being made a corporal. I have no medals and rely on my surroundings to identify the invisible spiritual aristocrat in me.

When I got back to Germany from camp, I still wasn't a private individual. I wasn't any Herr Timpe, Ferdinand Timpe. I was a returnee. You could tell that from looking at me, and I was treated accordingly. Lots of people were nice to me. They patted me on the back and said, "How now, Comrade!" Or: "Expect you've just come home, eh?" Or: "What was camp like, then?" They wanted to hear from me, or perhaps not. They called me "Du" and addressed me whenever and however they felt like. They felt sorry for me, or perhaps not—whatever the situation was, whatever they felt like. Their pity gave them a right to me, and I had to go on being something determined by other people. I was given a stamp and called "returnee." To be honest, I can't stand the word "returnee." It sounds a bit like the name of a vacuum cleaner or something. Something maneuverable. Gets in the corners and edges. It has something that smells of home and being looked after. Home for the homeless, home for fallen women, home for convicts, home for neglected children. Every time there's something to do with home, the bulk of people are terribly moved—by themselves. The victims that are sitting in it, they either have to play the role of the ungrateful object, or they permit themselves to be physically and spiritually castrated. The only sensible thing the moved parties have to give would be money, which of course they don't give.

I was on the train to Cologne and didn't want to be a returnee, just a perfectly ordinary private individual called Ferdinand Timpe.

I looked every inch a returnee. In the station waiting room in Cologne, I felt like drinking a glass of beer. A gaudy old bird joined me and wanted to take me and

my cigarettes. I gave her cigarettes and invited her to
share the bottle of schnapps I happened to have on me.
She wasn't a looker, but she was friendly and kind. As a
returnee, you can hardly expect a welcoming committee
of Roman courtesans. Anyway, I wasn't in the mood for
female consolation—neither by exquisite courtesans,
nor by a storm-tested ruin girl. Nothing drew me to my
fiancée Luise, either.

I set off towards the suburb of Nippes to my friend
Dr. Muck. In the course of my colorful life, I once took a
couple of semesters of German literature, till I couldn't
afford it anymore and settled down as an assistant ga-
rage mechanic. I learned some useful things there, and
might have stayed longer, had I not happened to inherit
a secondhand bookshop with a philately section. The
bookshop was in a little lane in the old part of Cologne
that didn't get much foot traffic. I led the serene existence of a hermit and lived quietly in the miasma of my
own mild wisdom.

I'd come across Dr. Muck at university. I hadn't seen
him for a long time, but I thought friends are for life.
Unfortunately, he'd married. Most men can't do friendship after they're married.

I got to chez Muck, and his wife answered the door.
She was sharp-featured and withered in a pinkish sort
of way. She spoke quickly and evenly. Initially she was
repulsed by my aspect, but eventually she let me in.

My friend Muck was away. Frau Muck was hosting a poetry evening that was like a religious service with a touch of sect. Under dimmed lights sat a goodly number of ladies with souls and serious expressions.

I was allowed to sit in a corner and was asked whether the ruins and above all the cultural devastation had not upset me. I had long since got accustomed to the ruins. Their aspect hadn't shaken me as much as was expected of me. My senses were numbed, and I sat there as in a dream.

But it seemed to me as though the ladies were somehow proud of the ruins. The way some women are proud if they've been through a dangerous operation. They don't like it if some rival in suffering comes forward with a still more dangerous operation. One of their great trumps is the sentence "The doctors had given up on me." In just that way the inhabitants of various German cities claimed that theirs was the one that was the most comprehensively destroyed.

On my way through the evening streets, I had seen the ruins in misty moonlight, and they struck me as charmed and eerily attractive.

Dear God, how much one had once had to give to see some piddling little ruin. When I was a boy, an old uncle dragged me through crowds, dust, and heat haze to some ruined castle on the Rhine, where lovers and trippers were taking pictures of one another.

Of course, I feel sorry for people who have lost their homes. We should all live in marble halls. I have never been moved by material losses. I am afraid of illness and of the loss of individuals who have put down roots in my heart. And sometimes I am afraid my heart may have become infertile ground, in which nothing and no one will be able to take root.

Maybe my capacity for suffering was low that evening with the spiritual ladies. I couldn't feel anything for the irreplaceable cultural goods either. One of the ladies was mourning a shattered church portal, and I had the sense that she couldn't have lived a single day without admiring its artful execution. Later I learned that the lady had never clapped eyes on said portal. Never apparently felt the need to either. When she went on to talk about five hand-embroidered cushion covers and three perfectly good bolsters that were stolen from her shortly after the end of the war, then her voice sounded sincere, and her grief seemed heartfelt.

I felt my want of empathy disappoint the ladies. I am sometimes incapable of thawing on the orders of fashionable imperatives.

I was relieved, therefore, when the poetic hour resumed. A stout lady in her prime called Herma Linde was reading lofty poems. I was unable to understand them. I tried to think. Is it possible to find incomprehensible things beautiful? Some people seem to find only incomprehensible things beautiful. Or maybe they kid themselves that they find them beautiful.

I was flagging, delicate mists fogged my brain. Out of the teeming haze loomed the form of a sanitary orderly I had once met. He had a large, mysterious boil on his hand. A handleless white cup from which I had once drunk rosé in Lyon. I saw the hairline crack in the cup. I heard the whinnying horn of a motorbike that drove past me in Amsterdam, and I remembered the grey rubble of a pavement in old Salzburg. A marsh marigold sprouted from it. I saw the laughing curls of a twittering girl who passed me once at a fruit stall where I was buying cherries. I saw the dark stain of rot on one Queen Anne cherry...

I was desperate not to fall asleep. Seven times I tiptoed out to the lavatory to take a sip from my flask. In the hall I walked into a sideboard and knocked over a large china ornament—I think it may have been a wood grouse. I broke off a piece of its beak. These things are always happening to me when I'm trying to be especially careful.

"Oh, never mind," said Frau Muck, in a tone of voice that told me she minded a great deal. She held the broken piece of beak in the palm of her hand, eyeing it with solemn grief. The other ladies also put tragic creases in their physiognomies. Other people may have faces, these ladies had physiognomies. I replaced the wood grouse on the sideboard. Why couldn't it have fallen noiselessly?

"Genuine Meissner," sighed a lady with tough russet curls. She seemed to have been assembled with rusty wires. They all stared at the debeaked wood grouse.

"The beak's not that important," I said, "other parts of the wood grouse matter more." I thought of the lovely feathers, but the ladies maintained a stern front, and one said the bird wasn't a wood grouse. To general sympathy, the lady of the house bedded the beak in a little box lined with cotton wool.

Outside, the ruins continued to bloom. I could see them from the lavatory window. I had retired there to commune with my flask and enjoy a few minutes' peace. The lavatory is the civilized man's only refuge. One isn't merely entitled, one is positively obliged, to lock oneself in. No one will ask you for statements, comments, confidences, kindnesses, accounts, sympathy, love, money, an opinion, enmity, friendship, or taxes, as long as you are in that temporary asylum.

I know children who read their first cowboy stories and young people who read their first love letters precisely there. I know poets who in such undisturbed spaces turned their budding rhythms into verses, and broody *penseurs* whose ideas came to maturity in the course of a few minutes of seclusion. The toilet is and remains the only place where husbands are free of their wives, fiancés of their affianced, debtors from their creditors, children of their parents, pupils of their teachers, and employees of their employers.

The time one may spend in the lavatory is limited, as all earthly happiness is limited. I am not one of those who would hang themselves in the toilet by their suspenders. I have neither suspenders nor a death wish. All I sought was a little peace, not to see or hear anything, no poems, no ladies, no broken-beaked wood or other grouse. If I'd stayed away too long, my absence might have caught the attention of the ladies, and they might have broken down the door. Lyrically affected ladies are apt to commit thoughtless deeds.

I looked for the drawing room and opened the wrong door. Wherever I am, I open wrong doors and set foot in wrong rooms. I'm not being figurative here. At the Mucks' I found myself in the kitchen. There on the table were three platters of canapés, some with cheese, others with ham on them. I ate a few without compunction, leaving gaps in the array of the smiling sustenance. Out of gratitude I decided to take my leave, to allow the ladies to eat something too.

This was in the time before the currency reform, when hunger painted many people's faces a yellowy-grey color. The poetry ladies probably weren't hungry, but they were maybe peckish. Spiritual feelings stimulate the appetite. In past times, I remember an unhappy love affair that made me a gourmand. Rarely did anything taste so good to me as then, when I was on the point of dying of my broken heart.

Initially, I was annoyed with Frau Muck for not telling me anything about the canapés. Then I said to myself, why should she? I had no right to Frau Muck, and no right to the delicious canapés. I reconciled myself to the situation. One must not expect pears from an apple tree, nor nuts from a pear tree, nor milk from a mole, and no milk of human kindness from a soul that's down-and-out.

I felt full and benevolent when I found the correct door. I returned to the corner of my sofa. Miss Herma Linde was still reciting. There was something priestessy about her. I am afraid of priestessy women. They have a grim, mild force and are strangely mean.

Wurmlauf der Elben, moderndes Gespinst.
Ernte des Grauens, wüstes Taggesicht,
Die Pracht der Leiche ward dir zugedacht,
*Was willst du noch? Ich neige meine Hand.**

I think this was from a poet who was still awaiting discovery. I pictured the priestessy one performing various humdrum tasks, swallowing a fishbone, say, or quarreling with the gasman.

---

* These parodic lines from Keun—who wrote poems as well—are like an amalgamation of Stefan George and Gottfried Benn: *Windings of Elbe, tattered thread of silk,/ Dread's dismal harvest, ravaged second sight,/ The corpse's full magnificence—gone!/ What more do you want? I extend my hand.*

The ladies waxed nobler, their sighs were so noble. I stroked a cushion whose silken threads got caught in the rough calluses of my palm. The atmosphere grew a little oppressive. I needed air. I had been intending to sleep at Muck's, but now I wanted to be gone. I would find some other shelter somewhere.

"I'm so sorry," said Frau Muck, walking me to the door, "I'm so sorry you can't stay, but why don't you come by next week. We are just forming a club for the protection of spiritually endangered individuals of this new era. We are striving to turn people's thoughts to the true and the beautiful."

From within I could hear Herma Linde intoning:
Chaos der Öde, Tigerin der Brunst,
Krampfender Schrei aus kahler Hufe Schlag,
*Nur hier und da ein Nabel aus Rubin.**

I felt I was in some fifth phase of puberty. "Might it be possible for you to lend me a blanket, Frau Muck?" I asked, because it was cold outside, and I was reckoning on sleeping rough.

Frau Muck had none. She had suffered so many thefts after the war, and it wasn't as though you could get new things either, everything was so expensive. "Those prices!" And then they had taken in her mother-in-law

---

* *Barren Sahara, tigresses' estrus,/ Stifled yawn or yell, the drumming of hooves,/ A belly button's not unexpected ruby.*

from Weimar. In the end, she let me have an ancient
lady's coat that smelled of mold, sweat, and mothballs.

To this day I don't know whether the coat was a gift
outright or lend-lease. I didn't think too much about it,
I cut myself a little tunic from it. Among other things, I
was once the right hand of a tailor in Marseilles.

What in God's name am I going to write? Something
has to give.

Thank God, something gave. Lilly just visited me
and bothered me. The pleasantest thing about work
remain the interruptions. I could write about Lilly.
Though I don't have much time, I have to go and meet
Heinrich.

Lilly is the victim of her beautiful feet. She studies
chemistry and earns money on the side from knitting
sweaters and writing. She lives with her grandmother in
two gloomy little rooms on our floor, at the far end of the
corridor. I'm not entirely sure how many people actually
live on this floor.

Lilly sometimes comes to see me when she's feeling
unhappy. Today she'd waited in vain for Konrad. Lilly is
often kept waiting in vain. She is a good, hardworking
girl, but unfortunately she's a martyr to her feet. She's
not ugly, you just don't notice her. The sight of her
doesn't make a man attentive and swivel-eyed. But she
does have strikingly beautiful feet. Beautiful feet are
rare in a girl. Someone must have said that to Lilly once.

From that day forth Lilly suffered a string of unhappy misunderstandings.

A normal girl wants to please a man. Girls with beautiful eyes, hair, lips, jewelry, clothes, have it easy. They can allow themselves to be desired and admired without risking anything. But what possibilities does a girl with beautiful feet have? She can go to the public baths. But summer is brief, and Sundays rare. The girl can't very well pull off her shoes in the tram, and she can't put her bare feet up on a café table without disagreeable consequences. Lilly is obliged to invite colleagues and acquaintances back to peppermint tea in her gloomy little room to make the most of her feet. And then she needs to take off her shoes and stockings. Men are apt to misunderstand it when a lady suddenly takes off her shoes and stockings in their presence—even if the lady is careful to say she is only doing so because she feels a headache coming on, or she can't breathe. There are certain gestures that seem to suspend distance, and it takes a powerful and controlling character to brush aside all unwished-for consequences with a smile. Lilly's is no powerful and controlling character. She encounters difficulties and inappropriate responses all the time. She is intelligent, even understanding, but she's always prepared to trample all over her reason—quite literally. With her beautiful feet.

Lilly came to me crying about Konrad. Unhappy girls are apt to talk rather wildly. I couldn't quite make

out whether Konrad had been overenthusiastic or chilly.
At any rate he hadn't been around today, and she had
waited for him till she felt ill. She is always prepared to
seek a lot of the blame in herself, and today she positively basked in self-reproach. She perched on the side
of my bed like a timid little mouse. I gave her a glass of
wine and she drank it trustingly, in grateful little sips.
With her hand she brushed the skirts of her little coat
and tried to lengthen it a bit. "Long coats are all the
rage," she said. Lilly takes all her feelings of inferiority
from her poor clothes, and all her confidence from her
feet. I wish her three corns and an ermine. The spiritual
change would probably do her good, and she might make
the discovery that changes are not necessarily either
good or bad.

I have to go now and see Heinrich. The fifty marks'
advance isn't what it was, and my article isn't done. The
result of my diligent labors is fourteen stories, none of
them longer than three sentences.

Heinrich was happy to see me again. "I do like your
name, Ferdinand," he said, and smiled at me with his
gentle eyes, "I do like the name Ferdinand Grossengrau." We had drunk a couple of cognacs by now, but I
didn't need to be reminded what my name was.

Ferdinand Grossengrau is a friend of mine. During
the war, we were in Berlin together the odd time. He is
an industrious poet, a doughty artisan of the word, boozy

as an old petrol tank. Heinrich had once met us two Ferdinands in an artists' bar in Berlin, between air raids. Our capacity for distinctions had already suffered, and we drank brotherhood as one does in the small hours, and to this day Heinrich has mistaken me for the literary lion Ferdinand Grossengrau.

Three times therefore in the course of the day I have met with recognition and appreciation—from the pickpocket, from Magnesius, and now from Heinrich. I shouldn't get conceited about it, though, each time the esteemer had mis-estimated. I should reconcile myself to the fact that my value resides in unaffected beauty and remains difficult for others to discern. At least I know my own worth.

Cousin Johanna

Today I am seeing Johanna.
"Ferdinand," she said to me
the other day, "I don't believe
in blood ties, and I don't quite
understand how we're supposed
to be related—but when push
comes to shove, you really are
my one true selfless friend and

my spiritual anchor." When Johanna talks that way, it usually means she's in danger of dying of a broken heart again. I don't know how many times a heart can break, but I think even the strongest and springiest heart won't survive continual breaking.

I don't know how old Johanna is. I lack the application and the feminine wiles to work it out. Also, I won't ask her straight out, because she would appeal to a woman's right to eternal youth.

Nor do I know how many times Johanna has been married. She always liked being married, and has made an unknown number of men happy, at least on a temporary basis. Even though she doesn't radiate the cozy comfort of an ancient sofa cushion and has nothing in common with the demonic sultriness of burgundy velvet curtains. When I think of Johanna, I can only ever think of wicked and sinful tubular steel.

Johanna believed there was only one great love in the life of a woman. Each time she was unshakably convinced she was experiencing it. Such emotional conviction gives a woman an optimistic freshness and elevates the chosen one to the status of a sort of super-eraser that rubs out and removes all who have come before him. Until someone rubs him out.

I admire Johanna's faithlessness. I don't see her as a loose, immoral person so much as a genius of forgetfulness. It's not agreeable to me when a woman has a loving memory, not since I was sentimentally bound to a certain widow. I would kiss her hair and say, "I adore your scent." (In one's younger days, one is apt to be shamelessly lyrical that way.) Nowadays, I don't think I would trust myself to say "your scent." "My Karl always used to find it exciting," the widow would reply, and we would have a long reminiscence about her Karl. How dotingly he would warm her poor chilly little feet on his string vest, and once, enflamed by passion, he tossed a hairnet in her direction. I am bothered by a woman's propensity to burden a loving present with unasked-for details of her past. I don't know if they do it out of an excess of communicativeness or in the hope of obtaining some propaganda advantage. At any rate, I only admire faithfulness in a woman if I am its object.

Johanna isn't short of ways of advertising herself, anyway. I can't tell if she's pretty or beautiful. She is ravishing. There are so many film stars and beauty queens who look ordinary to me. The majority probably take a different view, and my taste isn't representative. Certainly, though, Johanna has a je ne sais quoi—she electrifies like an eel. She has brown curly hair and wide, grey eyes. I don't trust myself to describe further details. That's usually how I am with people. I can see their face in front of me when I try to picture it—but as a whole. As soon as I try and remember a mouth, a nose, a pair of eyebrows, I'm all at sea.

Johanna looks like a mixture of Madonna, jack-in-the-box, and athlete. A Mary Magdalene too innocent to ever think of repentance. An angel who settles herself in Satan's lap when she feels the urge.

I think of the episode with her and the lion tamer. It was several years ago, and Johanna was rooming at the time with my sister Elfriede, studying something or other.

I have many sisters and many brothers too. Elfriede is atypical of us. She seems colorless and odorless, like some mixture of flour, water, and cardboard. She has a high opinion of herself and a low opinion of others, which makes life difficult for her. She is given to saying, oh, people are awful. I wonder if she counts herself? It's surely not pleasant to have a low opinion of yourself. Or does she think everyone else is awful, and not herself? That would condemn her to unendurable loneliness.

She married a minister who has a guilty conscience because he doesn't feel at ease in his calling. People with guilty consciences are apt to be severe. Elfriede's husband is the spitting image of his wife. Had they been missionaries, they could have converted cannibals to vegetarianism, they surely taste savorless and dull. They probably mean well towards the rest of the world, but they are lacking in tolerance. They are at pains to extirpate sin, the way a fanatical allotment gardener seeks to extirpate weeds. Some plants the allotment gardener thinks of as weeds are pretty flowers to others. What Elfriede and her husband take to be sins will be seen by others as things without which life would be unbearable. The result is a series of misunderstandings, and the well-intentioned extirpators get no thanks for their trouble.

Without any regard for her stainless relatives, Johanna fell in love with a lion tamer. There is no moral or physical force capable of tearing Johanna away from the man she is currently in love with. Naturally, the lion tamer returned Johanna's passion. He had no alternative. That's Johanna for you. Her lion tamer tamed his lions, she tamed her lion tamer—it was all a kind of chain reaction that a woman of Johanna's stamp surely found highly gratifying.

I once met the lion tamer. He was a friendly fellow with bandy legs. As a man, it is not given to me to assess the sex appeal of another man. The most striking thing about the lion tamer seemed to me to be a scar on his left shoulder that a lion had inflicted on him, Johanna told me about it. I wasn't able to see the scar, because we were in a crowded bar at the time and the lion tamer didn't want to undress. There was something coy about him.

Since those around her set their faces against her enterprise, Johanna's passion grew to gigantic dimensions. It is my view that the love of Romeo and Juliet was aggravated by the obstacles that were put in their way.

When Johanna is in love, she loves unconditionally. If the man in question has dirty fingernails and
sticking-out ears, then she will find nothing so charming as dirty fingernails and sticking-out ears. If the
man's a liar, she will find his imagination adorable—if
he's truthful, she will worship his simple nature. If
he is clever, she will be ravished by his razor-sharp
mind. Should he be stupid, then she will find his dull-
wittedness the essence of manly charm. It's impossible
to talk Johanna out of one of her passions by demon-
strating to her the beloved's flaws.

The episode with the lion tamer was viewed by Elfriede as wickedness and social slumming. Even though
Elfriede ought to know that our family has no claims to
social exclusiveness.

Suddenly, the air went out of the thing with the
lion tamer. He moved on when the circus left town. He
managed to write once or twice, but I have the sense
that his letters didn't impress Johanna. His qualities lay
elsewhere.

When the war ended, Johanna took over a lending
library, and she translates Italian thrillers for a pub-
lishing company somewhere in southern Germany. She
has always had several irons in the fire.

Behind her commercial premises, Johanna has a little bedsitting room. Recently, one Herr Peipel was to be
found hunkered there. Albert Theodor Peipel, inventor

and proprietor of Peipel's Pasta Products. A mature man with the beginnings of a paunch and dark, bulgy eyes. Johanna took to wearing her hair tidy and parted, and to being a sort of mixture of muse and needy lily. A muse, because Herr Peipel scribbles verses. He scribbles them for his noodles. Like so:

Peipel's noodles are the best
Both on weekdays and of rest.

Or:

Peipel's noodles make you sing
Ching chara a-ching-ching-ching.

Peipel's literary productions are clear, warm-hearted, and accessible to a wide readership. Nothing surrealist about them, nothing existentialist, nothing of biting satire. Peipel has a combination of simple nature and spiritual depth without which Johanna can no longer imagine existing. Not so long ago, she was on the way to becoming a disciple of Sartre and an enthusiast for Picasso's ceramics. The encounter with Peipel put her straight.

This morning I received a postcard from Johanna, with the wrong stamp and heatedly addressed. I was to come right away. I can't imagine the living creature that

would fall for the charms of the noodle-maker Albert
Theodor Peipel. But there are many things I am incapable of imagining that turn out to be the case. Perhaps
Johanna is tempted by the notion of being the first
woman to be destroyed by a passion for a noodle-maker.
Perhaps her subconscious is thirsting for the courage
to be ridiculous. Or maybe Herr Peipel lost his facility,
and for the sake of his art tried to murder Johanna. Most
murderers give themselves away by appearing so thoroughly harmless that no one would suspect them capable
of such a thing. I wonder how many times I have stood
next to a murderer on the tram, or at the bus stop, asking
for a light? I don't want to suspect Herr Peipel, but there
are poets who will do anything for a rhyme.

Johanna receives me, sparkling with joy. She has
changed. Her little bedsitting room is likewise changed.
She isn't wearing her hair in a tidy part anymore either,
it's the wild tangle of yore. The Virgin, the housemother
and muse, and the frail lily are all gone. She pours me a
glass of vermouth and seems terribly happy.

The change in the room I trace to the presence of a
nice little radio. I know Johanna has been after a radio
for some time. "Where d'you get the radio from, Johanna?" Johanna pets it.

"Where d'you think? From Meta, Meta Kolbe." I
am amazed. Meta Kolbe is an old friend of Johanna's.
Their friendship is lasting, since it is founded on mutual

dislike. Liking someone comes and goes, with dislike you know where you are.

Meta Kolbe is a homeowner, older than Johanna, blond like an aging Wagner soprano at the turn of the century, of blameless habits and anxious to marry. You can tell because she says, "I wouldn't change places with a married woman if you paid me to." Johanna assumes that Meta Kolbe advertises. Well, at her age you have to get a shuffle on. It wouldn't be right to console oneself with the knowledge that at ninety, Ninon de Lenclos was still passionately beloved.

Fräulein Kolbe feels drawn to Johanna. She finds her sinful and is waiting with bated breath for the moment when her loose morals come home to roost. Self-preservation means to some people that they retain a belief in earthly justice. For her part, Johanna has things to say about Meta Kolbe's devious libido and near-pathological miserliness. Hence my astonishment at the new radio.

And where is Herr Peipel keeping? Dusk was always the Peipel hour. Granted, Johanna doesn't give the impression of an abandoned woman. But then you get suicides living it up in the hours before their death, and all their friends say, "I had no idea, he even ate some pickled onions and fixed a mechanical pencil." I should like to know how intending suicides are supposed to behave.

"Is Herr Peipel not here then, Johanna?" I ask, even though I can perfectly well see that he's not.

"I prefer the radio," replies Johanna. To me, even a radio without tubes would be preferable, but coming from her the reply seems a little gnomic.

"When are you getting married?" I ask. "Never," says Johanna. "I've put that from my mind. Peipel may have some good qualities, but he's also the only son of an unprofitably married mother. Ferdinand, you can't imagine what that means. She's so resentful she gets ulcers and inflammations. She ties cat fur to his back, and wipes his nose for him, and is continually afraid he might get spoilt. Give me the radio any day." I ask her what Peipel has to do with the radio. "Everything," replies Johanna, "you see, I swapped him for the radio. I let Meta Kolbe take him, and she gave me the radio in exchange."

So that's the way of it then. I always took Johanna to be a stylish and imaginative woman. I wonder how she managed to palm Peipel off on Meta. I feel almost sorry for him.

"I whetted his appetite for Kolbe's properties," Johanna tells me. "Versifying noodle-makers are avid for real estate. And I whetted his appetite for her as well, I made up a different person. He was here a moment ago, and I sent him to her, saying I'd left my cigarette holder there. It's not true, I don't even own a cigarette holder, I smoke too much anyway."

"Well, and do you think he'll stay there? Won't he want to go back to you?"

Johanna beams at me. "Oh, Ferdinand, give Kolbe half an hour and she will have blackened my name to such a degree that Peipel will have forgotten all his serious intentions with regard to me. Believe me, she can do it." Such profound confidence in her friend, touching really. And the purpose of my coming was to check that things were going well, and to try and support the new axis. Johanna was a scrupulously honorable person, and she was resolved to exceed her obligations in return for the radio. She would also prefer Anton not to be disturbed by Peipel.

But who is Anton? Dreamy smile. It seems incredible to her that anyone in the world doesn't know Anton, and at the mere mention of his name isn't made happy and good. He just might be Johanna's first true love.

Johanna thinks there are people, even in our semi-enlightened epoch, who find her morals doubtful—just because those people have no understanding of true morals and true love. Johanna refuses to follow the path of such people. Bourgeois morality was looking to a woman for virtue and purity and it hedged her about with laws. Logically, an old maid, who had gone grey in the service of decency and honor, would be revered by young and old alike for the way she had sacrificed herself to the moral laws. Parents would queue to have their children blessed by the virgin's hand. But far from it, nothing good would befall such a wretch, says Johanna—all she was fit for was to be a figure of fun and a ridiculed old maid. "You know, Ferdinand, it's sad that there are still such foolish women who refuse to learn anything and have fallen for that morality nonsense."

Johanna pours more vermouth and balances on the arm of a chair; the radio plays hit tunes. Someone is singing "Kiss me at midnight." The voice sounds well bred, like that of a hotel guest asking a chambermaid if he could possibly have some fresh towels. I feel nostalgic for a gypsy violinist with a dark kiss curl, fiddling away in the ladies' ears and peeping down their fronts. Fire, but with discretion.

Johanna is telling me about Fräulein Rustikant. Fräulein Rustikant used to be Johanna's crafts teacher. Today she is seventy-five, sprightly and delicate as a bullfinch. A while ago she took to visiting Johanna. She was with her this afternoon and brought a bottle of gin. Fräulein Rustikant sat on Johanna's sofa, nimbly crossed her legs, lit a cigarette, and warbled her way through five glasses of gin. Her father had always been strict with her, and after his death, she had lived with her mother, who had been strict also, as had she herself. She came from a cultured family. During the war, Fräulein Rustikant wound up in strange parts, living with strange families. When it was over, she trooped back to Cologne.

She had made the acquaintance of soldiers, lorry drivers, vagrants, farmers. The house in Cologne where she lived had been flattened by a bomb. Fräulein Rustikant was taken in by a builder who had a small garden. Her brother in Ohio sent her CARE packages.

"She's as quick as a lizard in the sun," Johanna tells me. "The awful times weren't so awful for her. She's only sorry it didn't happen when she was younger. She wouldn't have minded having a man, even if just for one night—well, to see what it was like. And now it's too late. She says herself.

"You see, Ferdinand," says Johanna, "all the books and all the movies, they're all about love. Operas, plays, comedies, all about love. Voices from soprano to bass, love. Love in hit songs, love in poems, love in court reports. It's enough to make anyone curious. Trust me, Ferdinand, I wasn't exactly keen the first time it happened, but I felt I had to see what all the fuss was about. And then, by and by, I found out. And I have to say, I'm still learning. Now imagine a respectable creature, at twenty, thirty, forty."

"And sixty, Johanna," I say, "and eighty. It's going to happen to all of us unless we're dead first, and what am I to think of?" Johanna looks at me as though she wanted to brain me with the vermouth bottle. "Ferdinand, don't be ridiculous. Think of that person, getting older and more and more inquisitive. She's practically bound to

have an exaggerated notion of what love is, she's not
going to know how much or how little there is to any of it,
she's going to be driven mad by speculation. See, Fräulein Rustikant is going to be seventy-six next birthday,
and she doesn't know if she's gained something or lost
it. Renunciation can be a fine thing, Ferdinand, but
wouldn't you like to know what you're renouncing? I love
it myself."

"What's that you're renouncing, Johanna?" I ask,
doubtfully.

"Everything," says Johanna. "Or lots. Everything except Anton. I won't renounce Anton, I won't permit anyone to talk me out of Anton, not even you, Ferdinand."

I think people make their own beds in this life. I am
on the point of declaring to Johanna that one of my few
principles is never to interfere in other people's matters
of the heart, when Herr Liebezahl charges into the room
with the élan of a successful, overburdened businessman. Johanna greets him with fervent yelps.

Liebezahl is a good friend of mine, and someone
I owe a lot to. In Johanna's life he plays the invaluable
part of the amanuensis. Like me, he seems neuter and
endlessly employable. Liebezahl can easily afford to be
neuter on occasion. He is happy within himself without
needing to think about it. He is loved by, among others,
a genuine baroness with partly genuine jewelry. To Liebezahl she is a good customer. People he makes money

from he likes unaffectedly. He has a calm and selfless affection for a curly-haired blond girl who is studying medicine and who tosses around conditions the way Rastelli once juggled balls.

Her mother is a mailman's widow who assiduously kept the pair of them alive before the currency reform by black-market dealing. Her name is Maria, the mother's name is Martha.

Martha is flowering. Her muscles are blossoming. She used to steal coal, she heaved sacks of potatoes around, she smuggled in Belgian coffee.

There was one time she brought twenty wool blankets, five bars of chocolate, and a crate of soap into the wretched hole where the old people were hanging on without a home or a family to look after them. They were all hungry and cold. They had no friends and no one to love them. Children at least can be smooth-skinned and pleasing to the eye. Neglected children provoke interest and sympathy, including even from politicians. The abandoned elderly in their bunker had nothing to do except grow tired and die. If they happened to go outside for five minutes to sniff the air, then they would take in some light and strength as well, and the strength roused their almost exhausted capacity for suffering and hence extended their sorry persistence. Maybe it was wrong of Martha to bring them some joy and reanimate them.

Sometimes Martha paints her lips, and sometimes Herr Liebezahl likes her better than her daughter.

Liebezahl is a bouncy fellow somewhere between thirty and fifty, with a carnivalesque pate, a few scraps of fair hair, and boyish blue eyes.

In addition to Johanna's bedsitting room there is a further room at the back of her store, and that's where Liebezahl once based his enterprise. It's just a little branch office by now, Liebezahl has other, larger premises elsewhere in the city.

Liebezahl can do nothing and hence everything. His mission statement runs more or less like this:

Intimate of the stars and the magic of the cosmos. Cosmobiological institute. Interpreter of dreams. Graphology, chiromancy, science and magic. Get your subconscious raised here. Everyone is entitled to happiness and fulfillment in love, you just need to know how to go about it. Money is there to be picked up. Have your personality illuminated. No man is obliged to stammer. Nothing succeeds like success.

Liebezahl draws horoscopes, reads palms, swings crystals, lays cards, sells amulets, and does a little podiatry. He keeps extending his empire with fresh initiatives. Recently he opened a section on color that consists of a small room, painted white. On the walls are the inscriptions:

FIND THE COLOR OF YOUR SOUL.

KNOW YOURSELF THROUGH COLOR.

HAPPINESS THROUGH COLOR.

TELL ME YOUR COLOR, AND I'LL TELL YOU WHO YOU ARE.

HEALTH THROUGH COLOR.

Liebezahl had fifteen hand-towel-sized pieces of cardboard painted in fifteen different colors. He keeps his overheads low. "It would be helpful to know your color, Madame," he says, to a lady who has come about a corn or some occult matter. The lady is sat down in a comfortable chair in the little room. "Lean back, Madame, take the tension out of your limbs, relax." Liebezahl hangs up a piece of yellow card that the lady is then made to concentrate on for several minutes. It is followed by other cards in red, blue, green, brown, pink, and violet. The lady stares and stares. "Immerse yourself in it, Madame." The lady does so. "Fascinating, Madame, you are a fascinating case—I think we know a little more about you now." The lady would like to know a little more about herself now too. "What color do you find pleasant, Madame? What color makes you agitated? You are highly strung, such a pronounced orange type is rarely met with—we need to have you seeing more green. Five minutes of green, three times a week."

Liebezahl already has forty regulars. Ladies on their way to a social occasion drop in on Liebezahl first for their ten minutes of yellow or red, to be relaxed or stimulated. Others turn up in the wake of domestic ructions and partake of a little blue to settle their nerves. One tough-minded businesswoman comes five times a week to see pink, and to be helped to a sweetly youthful smile. She claims the pink has made her a better businesswoman. The wife of an official in the postal service assures anyone who cares to listen that three looks at carmine were enough to regain her husband's love. An intensive course of yellow helped an art teacher free herself of her depression and nervous stomach ailment. Eight men, including the owner of a delicatessen, a capmaker, and a barman, also belong to Liebezahl's faithful. As do I. When I was with Liebezahl yesterday, I said, "I'd like to see some orangey red and to be left alone."

Liebezahl removed the art teacher, who was engaged on her yellow: "There, that's enough for today. Too much isn't good for you." He led me into the room: "Here, Ferdinand—orange red will be pleasant for you, I'll look after you myself, make yourself comfortable, there are cigarettes on the table, I won't charge you a penny. I've just got in a very nice olive green..."

Liebezahl would have shown me all the colored cardboard I wanted. I looked at his olive green, then had some of the orange red, leaned back, felt nicely pampered. I was only bothered by the thought of the art teacher whose course of yellow I had interrupted. "Really doesn't matter," said Liebezahl, "I want to be rid of her anyway. She's starting to turn the color philosophy into a religion and calling me the new Messiah." I thought the publicity wouldn't hurt. "Too much publicity can," said Liebezahl, "and too much success is no good either." He knows what he wants. He left me to sell a customer some star-sign scent. The customer was a Capricorn who wanted it to take effect on a Scorpio. "This is a scent that never fails with Scorpio and Cancer, Madame," I heard Liebezahl say.

Liebezahl has various male and female assistants in his employ, but they lack his imagination and his persuasiveness. He is the life and soul of his enterprise, and it's rare that he can take half an hour off.

I asked Liebezahl once whether he really believed in his astrology and the rest of his mumbo jumbo. He was offended. Did I think he was stupid or something? It was enough for him that others were, enough to fall for that nonsense.

Some of Liebezahl's clients affect a superior smile, claim to be sceptics, and only to indulge in all this out of fun. Of course, it is precisely these sceptics that fall hook, line, and sinker for Liebezahl's magic. They remind one of people who ask to try morphine just once out of curiosity and go on to become lifelong addicts.

Across the way, three doctors share a set of premises. A neurologist, an internist, and an orthopedic surgeon. They have almost no patients. From their windows, the three doctors observe a steady stream of clients going to Liebezahl for help and advice.

Out of charity, and because his health is worth more to him than money, Liebezahl recently consulted the internist over a mild case of diarrhea. He referred one of the elderly color-lookers—who after three shots of purple had pulled Liebezahl down by the hair and tried to snog him—to the neurologist. He also tries to send some custom the way of the orthopedist from time to time. The doctors are beginning to value Liebezahl as a neighbor. A few days ago, the internist bought a little bottle of Capricorn scent for a certain lady and claims Liebezahl knows more than the neurologist. The neurologist in turn spoke deprecatingly about the orthopedist and went to Liebezahl for treatment of an ingrown nail. Ever since getting the purple lady as a patient, he has had a little money to spare.

Liebezahl is a helpful person. In answer to Johanna's appeal he horoscopically thrust Herr Peipel upon Meta Kolbe. He worked on Herr Peipel graphologically and made sure Fräulein Kolbe appeared among his cards. The two will hardly be able to oil out of their psychic destiny.

Herr Peipel is ashamed of admitting his belief in the occult mysteries, he plays the embarrassed fellow. But Liebezahl refuses to be fazed. He is certain he will have some decisive extrasensory impact upon Herr Peipel.

Meta Kolbe, meanwhile, is a true believer. If her horoscope predicted an accident for next Thursday, she would happily break a leg. Sooner a broken leg than lose faith in her horoscope. If Thursday brings no broken leg, then an ink stain on her finger will happily count instead. Whatever happens or doesn't happen, the horoscope is always right. It cost her money, and beyond that she is flattered that curious stars, moon-knots, dragons' tails, nebulae, and great and little bears are engrossed with her. She seems to picture excitable meteors, comets, Jupiter, and Saturn all out for a walk, making rhombuses for her, stepping into the third or the fifth house, and having a good natter about Meta Kolbe. "Hey," says a dapper comet, "did you see Meta Kolbe down there! Delightful person, the shyest sweetest little thing, but a dormant volcano. Some woman, though, eh? Let's sic Venus onto Mars a bit, I think she's earned it."

Johanna stuffs Liebezahl with a bit of liver sausage and some lemon sweets. She has an instinctive way of organizing menus. Liebezahl gulps down whatever is put in his mouth, his spirit is away elsewhere, his imagination is engaged. He is set on expanding his empire by a novel pairing of clairvoyance with fashion. He has been able to buy a quantity of striped and spotted materials from a bankrupt merchant. Now he needs a clairvoyant who among other things will let the ladies know that "I see happiness—happiness and dots—green dots on brown—silk—a man with roses—a large house—green dots—oh, it's fading..." Liebezahl likes the idea of an experiment where a clairvoyant will give fashion tips. "Madame," he will say, "that white blouse looks magnificent on you, and yet the weave is capable of absorbing certain disappointments. You see, Madame, materials have their own magic. The weave of your charming blouse won't let itself be imbued with your joys. It refuses the charm of your personality. It constitutes a barrier between you and the party to whom you feel drawn. Now, I have a clairvoyant, a material seer, who has made an analysis of fabrics. Would you like a risk-free consultation? I have a magnetic line in striped silk, which unfortunately does not work on every lady. I refuse to sell anything without the say-so of my textile magus. Perhaps you could come by next Wednesday, that is the earliest the gentleman in question could risk going into a trance."

"Will she come?" asks Johanna. "She thinks her white blouse suits her."

"But she wasn't happy in it," says Liebezahl. "Her white blouse let her down, the lady was looking to it for more effectiveness."

"How do you know she wasn't happy in her white blouse?" asks Johanna.

"Because she comes to me," says Liebezahl. "All the people who come to me are discontented and unhappy. Constantly discontented people are always stupid. Clever people don't come to me."

I have no pedagogical faculties, otherwise I might be able to persuade Liebezahl that it's more ethical to empty bins or open a skim-milk bar for recovering alcoholics than to put the squeeze on people whose lame mental mills are no longer capable of grinding the dull grains of their existence. But perhaps he makes people happier with his gaudy deceits than if he went around emptying their bins? Or else he would put a doughty binman out of work? You probably need a license to empty bins.

Johanna refills our glasses and rests herself against my bony chest. She feels the need for some fleeting animal security. "I will never understand, Liebezahl," she says, "how any woman could be stupid enough to fall for your gobbledygook—but you might let me have a yard of your brown silk with the green dots."

I am told to go and fetch Peipel and Meta Kolbe so that Liebezahl can work his magic on them some more. There's no time to lose, since he's got to go to Deutz tonight to meet Miro Rocca—that's the name of a clairvoyant and telepath who some weeks ago found a hidden coffee bean for some journal. Other magazines printed his picture. He

looked exhausted and despairing, just like someone with
newly depleted inner reserves would look.

I go the long way around, by the town woods, before
heading up to Meta Kolbe. I could use some fresh air. It's
not cold, and I feel at home under the misty autumn skies.
It does me good to be on my own. People alienate me from
life. It's been a while since I last stroked a tree trunk.

Meta Kolbe was alone, without Herr Peipel. She
offered me a small liqueur. Women like that give you
something syrupy when what you need is a bright, clear
spirit. Fräulein Kolbe looked rumpled and perplexed,
her bustling alertness seemed put on and unenthu-
siastic. Just as I was wondering how I might turn the
conversation to the matter of Peipel and the forthcom-
ing union, she raised the subject herself and asked me
what I thought of him. "A cultivated individual," I said.
She didn't entirely like him, said Meta Kolbe; admittedly, she was rather picky. (She struck me as the sort of
woman who would allow just about any remotely plausi-
ble male to make off with her savings book.)

"You put me in mind of an Italian painting," I said,
in an effort to perk her up. Women like to be told that
sort of thing. "Did you know you have remarkably beautiful temples? Did no one ever tell you that?"

"Oh, I don't know," said Meta Kolbe. I told her that
her nose indicated extreme sensibility, while the curve
of the corners of her mouth betrayed a demonically wild,

although carefully controlled temperament. "How could you know?" asked Meta Kolbe.

There is no sense in telling an upstanding woman that she's an upstanding woman, with gifts for frugal domesticity. She knows that anyway. Only a vicious woman likes to be told of her virtues. To a raddled old whore, I would say that she manifests a radical innocence and is at heart a simple housewife.

Briefly Meta Kolbe assays a conversation about developments in the Far East and recent American literature. She is relieved when I change the subject to the revelatory form of her wrists. She tells me about her childhood—"I was a hoyden, a real tomboy"—and her successes with the opposite sex, and why she didn't want any of them. The only subject that a woman will find interesting when talking to a man is herself. We went on to talk about Meta Kolbe's broken thumbnail, her first celluloid doll, her cousin's improper advances, her wandering kidney, her shy smile, velvety eyes, appendectomy, charm, preference for dry perfumes, health-food shops, roof terraces, Dover soles, tea roses, fur mittens, and Cossack choirs. Then Meta Kolbe started telling me her dreams. After the fifth, I took my leave.

I went off to report to Johanna on my unsuccessful undertaking. Evidently, Peipel had run away from Meta Kolbe, and I hadn't been able to gin up his memory. From her conversation, I got the impression that

Meta Kolbe might have been prepared to take me in part-exchange for her radio, if only I'd been ten years younger and twenty years wiser, as strong as the boxer Schmeling in his pomp, as sagacious as a cardinal, wealthy as a maharaja, and charming as a Hollywood star. I would have to work in the sciences, hunt tigers, lead daring expeditions, play the cello, write poems, master tax problems, be a political panjandrum, and spend all my days making love to her.

Someone who has suffered chronic nglect from the opposite sex must surely feel entitled to make a few demands of her own. As long as I can't afford to buy myself half a herring, I can keep the belief that apart from lobster in madeira, truffled pheasant, and baby asparagus I don't really fancy anything.

Many's the day I haven't been able to afford a tram ticket. I tramp along beside the rails, criticizing the cars that dart past me, occasionally condescending to spray me with muck. It's not the cars that are to blame—it's the rain, the poor state of the roads, and my ill luck as a pedestrian to happen to be walking past a juicy pothole just as a car with the naive and unquestioning confidence of a natural phenomenon happens to be passing. Cursing mildly, I hop up and down, and imagine the pathetic figure I would be had it been me at the wheel. Most of all, though, I criticize the cars. How few of them I would agree to drive. Mud-spattered from top to toe, I trudge on, imagining a winged Rolls-Royce, striking, elegant and discreet, shaped like a racing car and with the capacious comfort of a cozy old Citroën. When all the time I'd be happy to hitch a ride in a converted dog kennel with a two-stroke engine. The possession of this wheeled kennel would make me humble with so much blissful excess. As long as I have nothing, I won't just demand everything, I'll demand more than everything. Meta Kolbe is perfectly right to want a Hollywood actor plus prizefighter plus cardinal plus Bavarian yodeler plus exotic foreigner plus proper German plus dreamer plus businessman. She's right. She'll never find a husband, and I'll never own a car. The meanest and dowdiest would suffice for us, but we'll never get it.

When I returned to Johanna, I found a cheerful scene awaiting me. A friendly young man with enormous hands, jug ears, and a snub nose was playing the accordion. "This is Anton," said Johanna, "but you won't form a proper opinion of him, you need to see him from the back, he has a charmingly shaped head." It can't be an easy matter for a woman to maintain a passion for a man based on his rear view.

Peipel too is back. He is sitting in a corner with Liebezahl, receiving occult consolation.

Johanna drags me into her shop, we sit down on her counter, among the collected Ganghofer, some volumes of Rudolf Herzog, and a title called *Orchids, Blood, and the Amazon Basin*. "That's really popular," says Johanna. "The books that are most in demand are the ones that people think will be improper. I've got a title called *Sultry Nights*, and the clients queue up for it. But it's actually about humidity, it's set in the tropics or something, there's nothing about sex in it at all. People bring it back the next day, and they're too embarrassed to tell me it was a disappointment."

Then Johanna proceeds to tell me about Anton. He's a refugee from the East, he has an aunt in the West with a potato business, he's a brilliant accordionist who loves the samba and the jitterbug, doesn't read books, not even smut, and wanted to swap his wristwatch for a small electric heater to give her. The wristwatch is worth nothing, Anton wouldn't have got a clapped-out lighter, never mind an electric heater for it. But he meant well. "I could talk about him for hours," says Johanna.

"What about Peipel?" I ask.

Johanna makes a swishing gesture, knocking several pounds of Herzog, Gerstäcker, and Ganghofer to the deck. "I thought she was more sensible than that, Ferdinand. She was supposed to badmouth me, and she did, but she didn't do it right. She described me as a wild Messalina, a devil woman, faithless and easy. Who knows what all she told him. Anyway, Peipel comes trotting back all excited. Silly old Kolbe should have told him I had fallen arches and wear flannel underwear, suffer from chronic constipation, and am serially turned down, most recently by a widower with five children, because I smell of mothballs. If she'd said all that, she might have had a chance. The one thing she shouldn't have done is say I was sensual and immoral."

"What will you do about the radio?" I ask.

"You take it, Ferdinand," says Johanna. "Give it back to her. Anton's got his accordion, what do we want with a radio? If Peipel insists, I'll keep him by for a rainy day. Only I don't want him bothering me now, maybe you could take him with you when you go."

I packed the little radio under my arm. At the door, I said goodbye to Peipel. He said he was going to look for some mauve tulips for Johanna tomorrow.

I took the radio home with me. I don't quite trust myself to take it back yet; anyway, I think I should have a small reward for all my trouble.

I listen to music from a thousand stations. Johanna doesn't need it. Anton makes better music. Lucky her.

My fiancée Luise

Luise is living proof that the near panic in magazines and other official and unofficial organs regarding the preponderance of females is justified. I never thought it would be so hard to find a mate for a normal female creature. For almost a year now I've been deeply and futilely in search of a good solid husband for her. One might suppose that Luise doesn't need a husband because she has one in prospect already. Namely me. But that's just it. Luise has me. If Luise didn't have me, I wouldn't be seeking one so desperately.

Luise is a nice girl, and I've got nothing against her, but her presence has something oppressive about it for me. I have examined myself and established that this feeling of oppression is not love, and is no prerequisite for marriage, not even an unhappy one. I suppose I should tell her. But I can't.

There are three items that Luise managed to hang on to throughout the war: a stove, an electric iron, and me. All three of us are a little impaired, and not quite good as new. But Luise is hanging tenaciously, not to say grimly, on to all of us. Her favorite is the stove, and next, even ahead of the iron, is me. I would never deprive Luise of her inferior iron without offering her another, better one. How then am I going to take myself away from her if I rank higher than the iron?

I have trouble fitting into Luise's family life.

This morning I am so tired of people, I don't even feel like getting up.

I would like to be perfectly alone for a while. If you have no money and nowhere to live, you can never be alone. I'm not a misanthrope, and I don't want to be alone forever either, but just for a while I would. For many years I've been longing for such a time, and the longing has grown stronger, sometimes it even feels like a passion.

When I was a soldier, I could never be alone, when I was a prisoner of war I was never alone, and as a wretched returnee, still less so. Nothing against the Widow Stabhorn, who lets me live in her passage, and nothing against her thousand grandchildren either. They are splendid, optimistic people full of the will to succeed, and I am lucky to be in their midst. Only when I am with them, I am not alone. I am living in a sort of family association, and I would like just for once, and not necessarily for long, not to be living in any association. No family association, no provisional association, no national association, no professional association—not in any kind of association at all.

I had some nice comrades during the war, and some nice comrades in the POW camp. Only it didn't do me any good that they were nice, because the day came when I no longer found them nice and no longer counted myself lucky.

In POW camp pretty much everyone got on my nerves. I felt horrible on account of it, and people who make you feel guilty you of course try and avoid like the plague.

Albert, for instance, was a decent fellow and notoriously helpful, but I had moments I almost killed him with a billycan because he was sitting in front of me the whole time, picking his challengingly small nose.

Hildebrandt had backbone and a sense of humor. I admired him, and then forgot my admiration because Hildebrandt snored. He slept any time he had a chance to, even in the day, and he would always snore. He had a sophisticated and idiosyncratic way of snoring—willful, surprising, and unmelodious as the music of Bartók. Hildebrandt was a progressive snorer, and compulsive listening.

Hellmut never did me any harm, but he would eat with such an animal avidity that I felt the impulse to smash my canteen in his face.

Ludwig was an intelligent, sensitive soul. I knew that. But after he'd told me the same moronic dirty joke for the fifteenth time, I could only see him as a loathsome swine.

Some didn't tell dirty jokes, didn't snore, ate discreetly, didn't talk about women (or about men either), or about food, or politics, or about their release date, home, or the future. I didn't know them well, and I didn't think ill of them. And? I'd never have thought it—they annoyed me as well. They annoyed me by not annoying me. I was chronically unfair, and sometimes I knew it, and it made me sad.

Hence the relief of those individuals who were nasty pieces of work. I felt positively grateful to them because my rage for once was justifiable. Though God knows if it was always justified. I suppose I ought to thank those guys retrospectively for making it possible for me to be angry. When I think about it, bad people are actually martyrs. At their expense, you can find yourself virtuous, and give free rein to all your stopped-up feelings of rage. Where others are ugly, it's an easy matter to seem beautiful.

Back then, in POW camp, I came to thoroughly dislike myself. I got a grip and tried to appear cheerful and comradely to others. But privately my thoughts were tangled and ugly. My only comfort was the hope that I was just as infuriating to others as they to me. And I always, always wanted to be alone.

Even if I could afford to live in a hotel, that wouldn't be sufficient solitude. I'd have to greet the doorman, and the chambermaid would come to make the bed in the morning. They would wonder about me if I spent all day and all night shut up in my room. Their thoughts would come crawling to me through cracks, they would knock on my door, they wouldn't leave me properly alone.

I'm imagining a little room attached to a balloon high up in the sky. There would be a bed with me lying on it. Next to it a few essentials, drinks, cigarettes, and food. No one can get to me. Nothing around me but clouds. I have time. I could start to order my thoughts. Sometimes I think my brain is like an old bedside drawer, stuffed with all kinds of things I don't need. Maybe there is the odd useful item among all that junk. Maybe I'll sort it through one day. Or I'd be too lazy, and just jettison the lot. Maybe I'd do nothing but sleep. I might stay up there for weeks on end; then again, I might be ready to come down after a couple of days and find people charming and kind.

For the moment, my dream of solitude can't be realized—probably not in fact before I'm dead, and then I won't be able to enjoy it.

Now I need to go and see Luise and my in-laws. Oh, Christ. Luise happens to be my fiancée and in for a penny, in for a pound. (Idiotic saying. Why in for a pound if you're in for a penny? You could be in for a penny a thousand times over and never be in for a pound.)

I have yet to put up proper resistance to Luise. It's not really in me to be rough with mild-mannered girls in flowered frocks. Also, when I first met Luise, I was still less normal than I am today.

I was a young recruit in a small Moselle village in the early autumn, undergoing military training. When I was drafted, I resolved not to let anything get to me, to maintain an inner resistance, and remain dignified and independent. They can kill you, I thought, all cool and manly, but they can't do anything about your thoughts and feelings. Oh, but they could. After a fortnight, my

brain was no more capable of thought than an ancient
cowpat. The only thing I was sure about was that I was
going about everything the wrong way. My only feeling
was fear. I was swimming in an ocean of fear. I still don't
know why I had such irrational fear. It wasn't that I was
afraid of dying, I sometimes wished I could have died.
I was afraid of the NCOs, headquarters, uniforms, bar-
racks, corporals, the officers' voices—the whole massive
machinery of it.

I no longer saw human beings, all I saw were the mechanical manifestations of a force that hypnotized me to
the point of crippling despair. Sometimes I had the feeling that the world was split in two: one half was me and
the other was a huge mass of things, animals, humans,
whose sole objective was to harry and torture and mock
me. I was numb, I couldn't understand that others could
have such an influence on me. It was hopeless. I was
so terrorized I couldn't even cry anymore. Otherwise,
believe me, I would have. I was used to so much freedom
from when I was a boy, colorful, tender freedom. I knew
that poverty had edges, and life had rough edges that you
make yourself. But even they can be good. I knew forces
for good and ill, but I didn't know what force was.

I couldn't understand either that here were people
who weren't asking me to do things but telling me. That
I had to lie in the dirt when others said so, get up when
they said so, lie down in the dirt again, run, stand at

attention. I didn't understand it, I couldn't get it into my head.

I still can't. I don't know if other men felt and feel the way I do. When I did speak, I tried to speak like the others, it was a sort of camo language. Perhaps the others did too. Or am I a one-off, an anomaly, a psychopath festooned with neuroses who ought to be in a clinic somewhere? Damnit, I don't think I'm that unusual, and I don't think I'm crazy either. Which of course doesn't prove anything. Where's the madman who thinks he's mad?

It ought to be sufficient for me that my aversions are normal. They live in my emotions, and my reason says "very well" to them. Someone tells me he has a bad hand and needs my help. I would carry the coal up from the cellar and sew his buttons and empty his chamber pot and wash the dishes to the best of my ability. But if he started telling me to lie down in the dirt, jump up, do press-ups—then I'd smack him in the face, bad hand or no. Or I would suppose his brain was affected and start looking around for professional help. And when people start to tell me that military discipline is necessary for the preservation of a state, then I tell them where they can put their state. And if they tell me wars are necessary, then I am disgusted by whatever it is makes them so. Cross my heart, any power that forces me to fight, I hope they lose their shitty war.

I felt humiliated then, humiliated almost to the
point of annihilation. I obeyed without love and saw no
sense in my obedience. There is nothing so humiliating
as obedience without willingness and without love.

I wasn't a rebel. Good God, me a rebel. Then! I was
waiting in fascination for the moment when they would
next do something to me, when they just happened not
to be doing anything. How was I going to be able to do
anything to anyone else? I wasn't even capable of hating
another individual. They were all so impersonal to me—
the NCOs, the officers, the corporals, the pay sergeants.
They all shared one face, the angry face of the machine.

One time, a sergeant in the orderly room showed me
a photograph of his three-month-old baby. The man was
friendly. Not long ago I happened to run into him near
Johanna's lending library. "Willi Konte," he said, "remember? And you're Ferdinand—Christ, man, I knew
you right away." He was happy. I felt awkward, because
I wasn't happy. I wasn't afraid anymore of the sergeant
creature who now bore the name Willi Konte. I was just
afraid of hurting the rumpled, friendly, grinning man.
In my heart of hearts I'm a coward. I didn't want to take
him up to see my cousin Johanna, who might have adopted him into her collection. So I let him drag me to the
corner pub instead.

We drank beer and gin. The sergeant is working for
a roofer and is nostalgic for the old days. "It were great,

weren't it," he said, "let's drink to those days." The pub was freshly painted. The landlord had a new belly, which he was pushing along ahead of him shyly and proudly.

I remembered the baby photograph. I was bothered when the sergeant showed it to me. I thought: Is he playing a trick? Do I have to say, oh, he's adorable! Or am I *allowed* to say he's adorable! We're talking about a baby sergeant, after all. "You're a clever chap," said the sergeant in the orderly room, and held the picture under my nose and grinned all over his face. "You'll understand. Right? Yes?"

"Yes, sir, sergeant!" I replied, and hoped I'd done the right thing. The sergeant disgusted me because he was a sergeant. The product of his loins in the photograph was just as disgusting to me. The most disgusting thing of all was that someone was turning to me for human sympathy when he was part of the machine and represented the machine that was abusing me and violating me.

And now we were drinking pals, I was calling him Willi, and he was telling me he wasn't doing too well. "How's the kid?" I asked.

"I'm divorced," he said, "the kid's with his mum in Munich, she's about to get married again, anyway, what kid do you mean?"

I had no interest in Willi Konte and his divorces and his children. I remember him as a sergeant first class. He was a nice guy who wanted to show me the human touch. But I'd been with the army for four weeks and I didn't have any feelings anymore. I was growing scales. No nice guy was going to scratch my scales and stop their growth.

Sometimes I thought I should have committed suicide. I found my behavior inferior. "You're sick of life," I said to myself a lot. My still being around is proof that one is never as sick of life as one might think. One loves it. And what's with the "one" anyway? Who is "one"? One is neither I nor you. "One" is a copout for someone who doesn't have the guts to write "I." For instance, "One falls in love but rarely," someone says or writes. He doesn't want to say, I fall in love rarely. Or, you fall in love rarely. He wants to say I and you, everything and nothing, be vague and definite. The little word "one" is a eunuch word, you write it lowercase and take the decisive consonant away from it.* I resolve to try and say "I" more often.

Now then, I was honestly convinced I didn't love life anymore. But under mounds of dismalness my little life continued, wooed and worked for me and for itself. I wished I was dead, but I didn't kill myself.

I don't think I thought anything during my time as a recruit. Various terrors wipe out one's capacity to think, and hence one's capacity to suffer as well. One

---

* *Man*, the German impersonal pronoun meaning "one," is one letter short of *Mann*, German for "man."

can't feel without thinking—and one doesn't suffer without thinking. One! There we are again. Poor
castrate that I am. I take a huge run-up, puff myself
up front and back, race off with élan, and wind up in
cliché. From now on I won't say "one" again. I'll give
myself one more chance.

When I think of my time as a recruit, I ask myself
sometimes: How could all that happen? How was it
possible? I wasn't polite, but anxious to please. Not a
servant, but a lackey. I was the lowest and most abject
son of a bitch. A twenty-year-old lieutenant patted me
on the back and said, "You carry on like that, man." I
felt liberated and even honored by being patted on the
back by my benevolent young superior. I smiled gratefully, flattered.

Then one evening I was sitting on the banks of the
Moselle. Opposite me fluffy green hills intruded into my
view. The banks were crumbly, and I was a laughable figure. My head was shaved, and my reservist's uniform was
evilly ill-fitting. If I wore it today, I would reap the laugh-
ter of thousands at the Cologne Carnival. Back then I was
funny because I had to be. Not because I wanted to be.

Next to me on the bank sat a girl who wasn't laughing at me. Her name was Luise, and she was wearing a
flowered frock. I spoke to her, and she spoke to me. I was
tired and dull-witted and was relieved that I didn't have
to kiss her. The fact that I wasn't kissing her spoke in my

favor. I wonder how many relationships came about similarly, through such misunderstandings.

Luise wore a flowered frock, and she wasn't laughing at me. When I met her for the third time on the riverbank, the hills on the other side looked less fluffy and hostile, and I gratefully kissed her hand. It was a tough, willful little hand. I stared into space, the way I always did, and all I saw was maybe a bit of her knee and a scrap of her jolly flowered frock.

Once, I may have stroked Luise's knee, and another time I stroked her hair. Luise took that to mean that I desired her. And since I didn't do more than stroke her knee and hair once, quickly, she was convinced I was in love with her.

Her mother had misinformed her about love. "Men are only ever after one thing," she said, and "Only a man who knows restraint is capable of real love." At the time I didn't know anything about these lessons, and I allowed the decisive misunderstandings to come about.

I don't know when Luise began to view me as her fiancé. At the time I had a three-week furlough in that bloody little village on the Moselle. I expect it's perfectly charming, but for me it's a nightmare, even now. Even a paradise in which I was that unhappy is hell in the memory.

Luise was going to stay with her parents in Cologne Bayenthal. Before I went up the line with my company, I was in Cologne for a couple of days too. I still owned the little bookstore in the old town, my inheritance from my drunken old uncle. Later, three big fat bombs fell on it. It wasn't really necessary. Along with the rest of the building it was so rickety, a dud would have done the job. While I was living there, I only ever spoke softly, breathed quietly, and when I needed to sneeze, I went outside. All for fear of the place collapsing.

During my furlough, I once visited Luise at her parents', a courtesy call, no more. Luise had sent me parcels of some of her strangely tough homebaked cookies. I chewed on them, and then felt ungrateful because they were so bad.

Yes, and next thing I was sitting at her parents' place, at their coffee table, and I was her fiancé. I couldn't understand why these strangers were nice to me and seemed to like me. I could have run off, but I didn't want to give offense. Also, I was thinking, what does it matter, you might as well say yes to everything, you're about to go, and before long you'll be dead.

My father-in-law was an elderly gentleman who looked somehow plucked, with a dull, yellow forehead and mobile little eyes. He used to call me "our brave defender of the fatherland." He would say "we men" and "these are historic times."

He's a middle-ranking official. I don't know at what point one ceases to be middle-ranking and becomes a senior official, and whether a senior official is more or less than a top official.

His name is Leo Klatte, and the day before yesterday he was de-Nazified. "Re-classified as a fellow traveler," he told me proudly. I wonder who thought of the word "re-classified"? Can it satisfy the ambition of a proud German man to be a re-classified fellow traveler?

Luise is the Klattes' only child. Herr Klatte is a domestic tyrant. Tyrants resemble one another as drinkers resemble one another and vary as drinkers vary. What they have in common is the compulsion. Tyrants seek the intoxication of power, drinkers the intoxication of alcohol. To the unintoxicated, all intoxicated people look alike. They either avert their gaze, or they make way for him, as for a force of nature. Many people have a great yearning for a force of nature in human form. It's more than they can do at times, to continue to pray to the invisible and incomprehensible. They want God in a human body and wandering over the earth.

My father-in-law Leo Klatte is an amiable enough dictator. My mother-in-law Emmi is a gently weathered, slightly dippy blonde. She is afraid she will lose the respect of her fellow-beings if her lemon pudding fails to rise, and she feels violated if her carpet is stained. She has experienced everything, war and bombing and the destruction of her flat. Fortunately, she was able to move into the ground floor of the same building. During air

raids she would sit in the shelter and knit. When it got
to be very bad, she would lie down on the basement floor
with her knitting, and wail and pray. When the raid was
over, she would go upstairs and give the floor a much-
needed waxing.

She too had her great time. It is possible she may
have been a pirate wench in another lifetime and then
degenerated in the course of subsequent incarnations.

Shortly before the end of the war, Klatte was given
the rank of captain in an administrative position. For
the whole family that meant military glory and reaching
their social pinnacle.

As the war ended mother and daughter were by themselves in Cologne. They had stayed behind in their flat to
look after their handful of inferior junk. God knows, they
must have experienced some terrific bombing. If someone had told me years back that a pale, forget-me-not-blue
woman like my mother-in-law wouldn't simply die of
fright during a bombardment that felt like the end of the
world, I wouldn't have believed it. I would have bet all my
future happiness on it. Just as well I didn't.

The war finished, and Emmi Klatte took to thiev-
ing. The bombing had stopped, the artillery had packed
it in. The city seemed wiped out, destroyed. But some
things weren't. In the midst of the ruins there were a
few intact, abandoned houses and flats in pallid, ghostly

glory. Everything belonged to everyone. Insatiable and obsessed, my forget-me-not-blue mother-in-law went on the prowl, and snaffled among other things a sewing machine, various typewriters, four rugs, seventeen eggcups, a gilt frame, a bombproof door, a poultry cage, and a pompous drawing-room painting depicting a voluptuous woman lying prone in pink, puffy nudity, a blue moth teetering on the end of her pink index finger, and the whole thing somehow casual.

Before the currency reform the Klattes didn't know what to do for food. If a poor neighbor happened to receive a CARE package, the Klattes would have happily bitten her throat before the little wretch got anything down her, and it might have been worth it. Through my friend Liebezahl I took a hand. He bought the painting for some fantastic sum in reichsmark, before selling it on for some still more fantastic sum to a racketeer who put it up in his bar.

Whores cut up distinctly rough when you call them a whore. They don't even take it from other whores. Profiteers don't care to be hailed "Hey, profiteer." I know that from my cousin Magnesius. He is a periodic elementary profiteer. What he wants is to be called a businessman. I have no idea what the difference is between a businessman and a profiteer. It's possible that people who have come by money have at the same time acquired sensitivity and care about labels. Perhaps it's all in the way it's said, and it's down to me if some future Rockefeller feels flattered or offended if I say to him, "How's it hanging, you old crook?"

My mother-in-law was reluctantly parted from the painting. She wasn't even pretending when, with tears coursing down her cheeks, she told Liebezahl that it was an old heirloom that had been in the family for generations. Since then, the former owners have appeared. "Awful people," said Frau Klatte, "not even properly married. People who own such a vulgar piece are bound to be suspicious—and the fact that they want it back, well, doesn't that say everything." The fight over the painting has been going on for more than a year, and no end in sight.

For five days my mother-in-law went on the rampage. She slaved away like a coolie and developed the muscles of a removal man or a prizefighter. Novels teach us that when faced with adversity or opportunity, women are capable of developing uncommon strength.

Emergencies, though, by their nature, don't last, and Frau Klatte lapsed back into her housewifely existence.

Herr Klatte reappeared on the domestic scene, stripped of his heathen glory, looking, in fact, rather bedraggled, like a cock that has had its tail feathers plucked. He was wearing the timeless mufti of the middle-ranking official. Previously the narrow waist and the splendid epaulettes of the officer's uniform had lent him a breath of intoxicating virility. Not long ago, he hinted to me, "man-to-man," that he had cast a powerful spell on the widow of a stationmaster. Later, the rail widow had offered her favors to an American sergeant who was still in victorious possession of his uniform splendor. "Don't talk to me about German womanhood, I know all about it," said Klatte bitterly. "I've had it up to here with politics."

He settled down among the spoils of his wife and pouted. His wife and daughter waited on him, the household was his to command, and gradually he clambered back up to the temporarily vacant throne of the family dictator, and everyone tried to be as satisfied and dissatisfied as they'd been previously, in the good old days.

I never understood why some of my erstwhile comrades were so angry with women and girls who liked Allied soldiers. My God, hadn't they dinned it into the poor creatures that the uniformed, powerful, victorious hero had to be the woman's highest ideal? What was promulgated was this: the German wins, and whoever wins is German.

In a Rhineland village I talked to the owner of a haberdashery—a woman whose understanding enabled her to cope with her life.

The Americans marched into the village. Slowly, reluctantly, but victoriously. The woman was full of joy. The victors gave her Camels, and she gave them the victory palm. In a manner of speaking. After all, this is Germany, not the Sahara. "The Americans won," she said, "so they must be German, and we must show our gratitude to the gallant victors. The general's name is Eisenhower, which is almost a German name."

What was I to say to her? You can't make women support a war without enthusing them about heroes and fighters. They were supposed to love the smiling victor, and they did. Many women who had been successfully trained to be enthusiasts for the war and worship the heroes later degenerated surprisingly quickly in their national feeling. They couldn't help whooping at the victor. The pacifist's sexual compassion for the defeated had failed to develop in them. The infantile joy of the woman at material things enabled her to bloom for the victor in heart and senses.

My bride Luise is among those girls whose virtue could not be impressed by Nescafé or chewing gum. She didn't fall for the charms of the alien conqueror or for the continual siren song "Hello, Baby!" that rang out through the ruins of the postwar months in Germany.

"I have remained faithful to you," Luise said to me just at the moment I was going to suggest ending our engagement and parting as friends. "I have remained faithful to you, Ferdinand, you can be proud of me."

"Thank you, Luise," I said, and I felt mean and low, because I wasn't in the least grateful. To lighten my bad conscience, I threw myself on her old stove, to repair it. I didn't dare suggest breaking our engagement.

A girl like Luise deserves a better man than me. I haven't given up hope of finding her one. Thus far, I have felt obliged to go on painting the walls in Luise's flat, fetching firewood and coal, repairing wiring and toilets, looking after the allotment, fitting cellar doors and windowpanes, knocking together furniture, and pickling cabbage. Something new every day.

More than every mountain in the world I love the sea. I often plan to go to some fishing village. Maybe I could help some old fisherman fix his nets and bring in the catch. I think I could. I once lived in Brittany for three months, without a penny.

I told Luise of my plan, and that such a rough and uncertain existence was unsuitable for a sensitive woman like her. "I will go with you," said Luise, "I will share your burden." We had seen a film together a few days previously in which the hero throws himself at the violent bosom of a still-unspoilt nature. The doting heroine follows him. Leaving behind her the world of nylons, beauty contests, and New Look, she waded through

the storm-tossed dunes to an almost naked collapse.
And everything came up roses. She was carried into a
handy fisherman's hut in the strong arms of the hero. He
warmed her delicate limbs, and before long there was
a merry blaze in the hearth. Dreamily the lovers stared
into the crackling logs.

Luise had been impressed. Goddamn the cinemas of
the world. How can I go on planning to move to a fishing
village, without having to fear persecution? Each time
I trod on something unusually soft in those soft dunes,
I would have to think, you are stepping on the earthly
remains of your loving bride, who lost her way as she
tried to follow you. You are stepping on the victim of your
brutal, cowardly, manly egoism.

"Mum always says no man knows how much a loving
woman sacrifices to him," she said at the end of our
conversation about the fishing village. I was happy that I
had curtains to put up, and the stovepipe to take out and
clean.

While I was busying myself with the dirty stovepipe,
Luise tooted from the next-door room, "You don't even
have a permanent job, but I'm sticking by you, I'm your
steadfast little Lu."

It had always bugged me when she signed her letters
like that: "Your little Lu." She's a big solid woman. The
role of the little chickadee doesn't suit her.

Maybe I will manage to find a man who likes her. I've got to. If Luise takes him, I'll happily continue to clean sooty stovepipes, even though it's ghastly work. I promise also to weed the garden, put the sheets through the mangle, help the hens lay, and wash the nappies of the babies.

Unfortunately, we're not at that stage yet.

A husband for Luise

Tonight, I am going to see
Luise. My father-in-law's re-
classification as fellow traveler is
being celebrated. The day before
yesterday he was de-Nazified.

Before that I have to see my
friend Heinrich, the editor of
Red Dawn. I think his first issue

still hasn't come out. The story he asked me to write isn't written yet either.

I'm going to take Heinrich to meet Luise. He is a bachelor and could use a wife to stand by him during life's storms. Heinrich is a mild-mannered intellectual, shy and a little unworldly. Not one of those aggressive ironists. He is a man who would believe a barmaid every time when she's telling him how her father was a senior officer who went broke, how she had had an old-fashioned convent upbringing, detested sin, and was consumed with anxiety for her little old mother.

Never would Heinrich walk into a bar by himself, though one could imagine a more frivolous colleague dragging him into one. He doesn't resist much. Occasional visits to nightclubs have given him insights into the lower depths of the human psyche. The most hard-boiled waiter can move him to tears by telling him how he had to serve several years in prison because of his attachment to an old canary. He had committed a serious burglary because he saw the critter wasn't getting any seeds.

Of course it's not entirely altruistic on my part to try to produce a connection between Heinrich and Luise. But I do believe that she could be useful to him. She would acquaint him with some of the realities of life. She would be a good counterweight for him. Abstract thought isn't her thing; she's the opposite of a bluestocking.

She will occasionally dip into a magazine. Ideally some story about a tragic film star, youth criminality, cake recipes, or glamour tips. She is interested in the latest mass murderer, the practice of suttee, rapes, storms, and astrologically based predictions of catastrophes.

Luise and her mother are just now waiting for a comet that is reliably expected to collide with our planet in the next few days, with consequences unknown. My landlady Frau Stabhorn was full of news concerning the coming calamity as well. She reckoned there was nothing to be done about it and was more interested in her currently rather sticky jam business and a bottle of Armagnac that a son-in-law had gone and drunk. Single widows don't have an easy time of it, they are used to worse than collision-happy comets.

Luise has a weakness for newspaper quizzes. I devised a couple for Heinrich, maybe he'll pay me for them. I showed him this one:

Our reporter was instructed to ask forty-seven males the following question: do women with facial hair have sex appeal? Nineteen replied in the affirmative, among them a tram conductor and a noted movie actor. Seven preferred unshaven women, three volunteered that they cared more about shapely legs than hairy upper lips. A chimney sweep

claimed a woman could have sex appeal whether or
not she had facial hair. A retired lower court judge
thought facial hair and sex appeal were compat-
ible, given a personal fortune and an agreeable
character. Only one elderly watchmaker asserted
that a woman with facial hair could arouse noth-
ing beyond comradely feelings in him.

Heinrich was unpersuaded by my efforts thus far.
Editors never know what they want. They don't have
any personal taste of their own, and if they do, they will
stifle it for fear it may not coincide with that of their
readership.

I have a further quiz I'd like to try: "How do I get rid
of my fiancée?"

I've tried asking many acquaintances. My cousin
Magnesius couldn't understand why I would ask such
a thing. He reckons that any woman would happily run
away from a worm like me. He gave me to understand that
several gorgeous women he had scorned had gone on to
attempt suicide. "Main thing is, don't get soft," he said.

Heinrich said he would give a woman he'd left a job
as his secretary and continue to offer her moral support
and friendly advice. That's not the same as being rid of
her. She will go on loving and suffering.

Liebezahl had a think when I asked him. "It's easy to
get rid of a fiancée," he said, "you probably mean a loving

woman whom you don't want to hurt?" That is indeed
what I meant. Liebezahl reflected on the possibilities of
astrological deterrence. They seemed inadequate to the
purpose. "I would grovel to her," he finally said, "I would
give her the lovelorn swain for so long that she would
eventually think I was entirely ridiculous and have
enough. I would make her overweening and peacock-
like. One day she would leave me."

I think the Liebezahl approach, while humane, is
slow and a little uncertain.

I would need to know what a woman sees in a man,
and then seek to project the opposite. I don't think
women are brave enough to try the same thing on a
man. I was always suspicious when women lamented, "It
doesn't matter what I do, I can't seem to get rid of him."
All they would need to do is be in a constant tearful sulk,
neglect their appearance, dress in tasteless and ridiculous styles, smell bad, scratch their scalps with their
forks, pick their noses, bad-mouth other women, tear
buttons off the man's suit, and burn holes in it with their
cigarettes. I am convinced that a woman would be shot of
the most devoted lover in short order.

It is my hope that Luise will one day turn her back on
me in disgust. Today she is meeting Heinrich. Heinrich
has money, Heinrich is hardworking, Heinrich is gentle
and affectionate, he is well brought up, both bourgeois
and high-minded, positively elegant in demeanor, and of

stainless appearance. In skat terms, he would be a jack
of spades while I'm the seven of diamonds. Admittedly,
jack of spades down is worse than seven of diamonds
in the hand. Unless, that is, Luise played *nul ouvert*. But
then I think women would rather play a grand in a four-
some. Besides, they don't know how to lead, they always
overdo it.

At the Klattes', the festivities have begun. Luise's
cookies have been baked according to a magazine recipe:
aromatic and without butter. I've met their sort before,
and I avoid them. If I should lose an eyetooth, I don't
have money to buy a new one.

To raise the general spirits, there's punch to drink.
Everyone has chipped in. The Klattes donated two bottles of sour Moselle, Johanna a bottle of still more sour
Ahr wine, Heinrich a bottle of sekt, and I a half-bottle
of domestic cognac, which is so bad that Frau Stabhorn
let me have it on credit, purely to be rid of it. I poured
the lot into a fish tureen and gave it a stir. It couldn't be
worse than the sum of its parts. I called the whole thing
a champagne cocktail. A label can make anything taste
better. Now—after the third glass—no one has the least
idea whether it's good or bad. Before the currency reform, we drank stuff that no yogi could have withstood.

Heinrich is in fact just talking about a yogi who is in
our midst. He is terribly impressed with the fellow and
would like to publish an article on him in his paper. The

man is nothing short of miraculous, a medical miracle. You can hammer nails through his tongue and he doesn't bat an eye, drive long needles through his body and he doesn't bleed, bury him for hours on end and he doesn't suffocate.

Johanna would like to meet him. The Klatte ladies are faithful, impressed, and anxious to hear more.

My father-in-law feels it incumbent upon himself to assert his authority through skepticism. "Women are apt to fall for stunts like that," he says. Frau Klatte feels offended by the word "women." "What do you mean, women? You men fall for stunts just as much, you fell for Hitler's stunts, Leo, otherwise we wouldn't be celebrating your de-nasty-Nazification today. Golly, that word is hard to say."

A withered anemone in the hand of a child is like a tiger compared to my mother-in-law in the grip of day-to-day living. But I keep seeing how that delicate, oppressed female harbors dormant forces that can be roused to splendid awakening by means such as states of emergency and champagne cocktails.

So as not to allow the festivities to become tarnished by politics, I change the subject away from de-Nazification and back to the yogi. Women are devotees of supersensory phenomena and find terms like "old Indian Tantric cults" intoxicating. Heinrich looks suddenly devout as further yogic miracles are described. Klatte capitulates and plays the cultivated fellow, quoting the Swan of Avon: "There are more things in heaven and earth than in thy philosophy, Horatio."

I sigh with relief when the quotation comes. It had to come, it was overdue. As soon as the attention of a group turns to matters inexplicable, it's only a matter of time before someone, full of weary wisdom, drops it into the conversation to stop everyone else from pushing more things onto the astral plane.

Johanna refills everyone's glasses, the yogi talk has died the death. Luise fiddles with the wireless and finds an opera she thinks might be *Il Trovatore*. Klatte insists it's *Tosca*, Frau Klatte reckons *Oberon*, Johanna plumps for *Aida*. No one is interested in listening to it, but now everyone is waiting for it to end so that we can hear what it was. I am too unmusical to become involved.

I am left thinking of the lamentable irrelation between the attainments of a yogi and his earning power. What's the point of such a man's superhuman gifts if there's nothing he can do with them beyond earning a crust at a funfair? Any bank employee has a better life. What makes a yogi a yogi? It can hardly satisfy any artistic or intellectual ambition to walk barefoot over broken glass, have yourself buried alive, or get some other hideous thing done to you. Even his powers of hypnotism hardly take a fellow like that any further.

On the other hand, how impressive and convincing it would be if a yogi walked into an expensive restaurant where people like Cousin Magnesius were dining on trout and smoked goose breast. The yogi would coolly stop in the entrance. Slowly all the movers and shakers would lower their eating irons, walk up to the yogi, and, bowing deeply, put down their wallets. The snooty headwaiter would pick them all up and hand them to the yogi. Too bad I'm not one. Nature far too often squanders talents and aptitudes on the wrong people.

Johanna is singing a flirty American hit song. I'm not sure if she's drunk or just playing drunk. The Klattes eye her askance, and that's as well. The reason I asked Johanna along was to show me in a poor light. Luise is to become convinced of my worthlessness and so be deflected to Heinrich. I planned the whole thing with considerable acuity and psychological insight. I give Johanna an encouraging nod.

Johanna is telling us about Jimmy, a charming American soldier she met in the summer of '45. Luise frowns. "Why ever not?" says Johanna. "I wanted an American soldier for myself. I had a letter from him the other day, he's in Texas now," Johanna tells us. I know the story. One could call it something like Johanna and the White Rose, a ballad in prose.

It was the summer of '45. Sun, ruins, confusion, and dirt. Johanna was sleeping on a mattress beside the

ruined counter of her present-day lending library. The
rest of the room was in pieces, but by the standards of
the time was accounted in quite good shape. One lunchtime, Johanna was carrying buckets of water from the
other end of the street. An American GI called out his
"Hello, Baby," and helpfully took the buckets for her.
Johanna had long curly hair, dramatically pale shrunken
cheeks, a simple dirndl dress, and round, innocent eyes.
In the association with the buckets of water, the overall
effect will have been like a popular song. The soldier
was called Jimmy, and Johanna thought he was nice. He
suggested coming by later, and Johanna was looking
forward to some proper ground coffee. She had been
told that the prime purpose in life of American GIs was
to scatter ground coffee among the population, and she
fancied some. She enlisted Liebezahl for the evening,
because he speaks English and could get hold of a couple
of bottles of wine.

Liebezahl turned up with the bottles of wine and
a German–English dictionary. Jimmy didn't. Not at
six, not at seven, not at eight. Johanna was annoyed
because of the coffee, and just in general. At nine
o'clock, Jimmy turned up, a little flushed, but beaming. He came conservatively, bearing a white rose. He
had spent hours wading through the ruins of Cologne
till he found a white rose for Johanna. Other than the
white rose, he had nothing, no coffee, no cans of meat

or beans. He told her over the course of the evening
that in his mess they were drowning in coffee, which
he didn't drink anyway, and he had had it up to here
with canned food.

Johanna didn't mention the coffee. She made an
inner adjustment and was delighted by the white rose.
Cautiously, she put it in her only water glass. She drank
her wine from a cup without a handle, while Jimmy the
Rose was given a tin can, and Liebezahl drank straight
from the bottle. The evening passed off merrily and
peaceably. The white rose shimmered and smelled
faintly. "Poor old Europe," sighed Johanna, "it's not even
a romantic continent anymore, now we even import our
romance." She gave Jimmy the eye, but he didn't understand, and Liebezahl is neither romantic nor introspec-
tive. Later on, through the agency of Jimmy the Rose, he
was able to pull off a few lucrative swap-deals.

That evening, though, everyone was gentle and
dreamy. The moon rose. Jimmy's eyes were a beaming
nursery blue, and Johanna sustained herself through the
feeling that he liked her.

The next morning, she scraped some beet jam onto a
crust of bread, drank water from the cup without a handle, and tried to draw sufficient optimism from the sight
of her white rose to be fit for the day ahead.

For my sake, Johanna adds a vague, shimmering conclusion that leaves open certain obvious

possibilities. Even so, the Klatte ladies are not sufficiently indignant. The Romance of the White Rose made a favorable impression.

My father-in-law tells Heinrich anecdotes from his time in the army. Tortured but attentive, Heinrich listens. Everything the Klattes say is important and revealing: they represent his future readership profile.

I have another drink. My brain is clouding over, and the world is growing alien to me again. I don't feel at home in myself. Luise has a new hairstyle that suits her. She is a nice girl. Too bad I don't love her. The older Klattes are nice to me, but what are they to me really? Probably they see something in me that I am not. But who can prove to me that I am what I think I am? You meet a thousand people, and they will take a thousand different views, and your own is the thousand-and-first. It's confusing to think about how multiple and various you are. When I think about how many times I exist, I have to wonder whether I even exist at all.

I feel so deep-frozen. I wonder if I'll ever thaw out in this life.

At least other people have some kind of ambition, a little illusory fire at which they can warm their hands. What have I got? Sometimes I feel like wandering on through the entire world. Maybe eventually I'll run into a place or a person who will make me say yes, this is it, I'll stay here, this is my home.

I wonder if it's the punch, making me melancholy.
I must take steps against it. Thomas Aquinas recom-
mends baths and sleep against low spirits. If the Klattes'
gas water-heater hadn't been broken, I might have tried
to take a secret bath this evening.

Everyone is lively, the conversation is washing
around me. They are talking about Hitler. Just now a load
of German newspapers are carrying articles about him
again. An acquaintance of Eva Braun's writes, Hitler's
personal attendant writes, Hitler's secretary writes, a
mailman, a general, a movie actress write. I have no
interest in Third Reich gossip. Personal articles bore
me because they usually favor the person writing them.
Just at the moment there seems to be a vogue for them,
though. I can see that Heinrich would love to print
something of that sort. Maybe I'll write one for him: I
was Hitler's pest control guy.

An agitated ringing interrupts the conversation.
Luise hurries to the door, and two energetic-looking
women stream into the room. We can tell right away
they have come with unfriendly intentions. Since they
both speak at once, and further, keep correcting one
another, it takes some time for the purpose of their visit
to become clear. They are demanding the return of the
bombproof door, and a window frame that they claim
Frau Klatte illegally took from a half-destroyed house.
The Klattes are gradually getting used to such visits.

People still drop in wanting this or that thing that Frau Klatte stole. Of course, Frau Klatte resists. What she has she holds. It's quite possible that people feel more attached to things they have personally stolen than things they have honestly acquired. All the Klattes are firmly convinced that things that have been in their possession for years belong to them.

When he has been drinking, Herr Klatte occasionally suffers from attacks of universal philanthropy. He asks the women to stay for a drink. In carnivalesque exuberance, he produces a further bottle of spirits.

To begin with, the women aren't interested in staying or drinking. Mention is also made of a handcart that has been left outside the door that is liable to be stolen. "We're all honest people here," says Herr Klatte, and asks me to wheel the cart into the entryway to set the ladies' minds at rest.

The ladies give up their resistance and join in the general festivities. Perlbaum is the name. Luise passes them some of her home-baked goods, Johanna puts asters in their hair, Frau Klatte asks if they wouldn't prefer some bread and cheese, and Heinrich asks them what their favorite reading is. He stares in ravishment at the unpretentious ladies of the people and tries to divine their literary preferences.

The radio plays a carnival hit, and this affirms the conciliatory mood. The Perlbaums wax enthusiastic

about *Weiberfastnacht.** What else was life good for,
everything was much too expensive, and where was it all
going? Frau Klatte is fully in agreement.

Johanna remembers the conditions of her coming
here and starts flirting with me. It would take a real
expert to tell it from the genuine article.

I see Luise smoking; there is ash on her dress.

The Perlbaums want the return of their bombproof
door, because the world is supposed to end the day after
tomorrow, and ideally they would have the window
frame installed as well. Frau Klatte isn't convinced
about the end of the world, but just in case she'd like,
with Luise's help, to set the washing to soak. Then she
tries to find out what ill-intentioned individuals set the
Perlbaums on her track.

Heinrich is keen to publish an article on the end of
the world. If it's not happening, I won't have much to say
about it, and if it does I'll have even less.

The Perlbaums aren't opposed to the end of the world.
No reason why they should be. The world's not up to much
anymore, there's lies and deceit wherever you look, there
were plenty of bankruptcies in the summer, they wouldn't
vote, politics were evil, prices were much too high, they

---

* *Weiberfastnacht* (Women's Carnival) is held on the Thursday before Ash Wednesday in Catholic parts of
Germany, including the Rhineland and (as here) Cologne; in the course of riotous celebrations, women
are free to kiss men on the cheeks and to chop off their neckties.

had a nephew who needed something to wear to his confirmation, but dark-blue suits were so unpractical.

Frau Klatte and Luise haven't had to go hungry since the currency reform, in fact they've each managed to put on around fifteen pounds. Surely they would agree things are going better for them.

Then, full of quiet reverence, I recall the great day I had not long ago. For the first time in years, I threw away a cigarette end quite reflexively, without even thinking about it. Afterwards I felt almost guilty. I hope my little fit of irrational exuberance doesn't come back to haunt me one day.

My life as a smoker was one continual remorseless descent. One day on the train I saw a well-dressed gentleman who didn't throw away his dog end, but carefully dinched it and stuffed it in a box along with other dog ends. They looked distinctly unappetizing, and I shuddered. I thought to myself, admittedly, I'm a smoker, but if I'm ever reduced to that, I'm going to give up. There are limits, and even the worst addict must muster a minimum of self-respect.

A few months later, I was collecting my own ends in a little tin. Once I was sure I was alone, I pulled out the threads of tobacco. A few weeks later, I no longer cared if I had witnesses to this.

Then, in a pub, I saw a man pick up strangers' cigarette ends from a strange ashtray. I was revolted.

Everything must have limits, I thought. It's only natural that a man will smoke his own stubs. But to seek out those of others is degenerate. I'd sooner give up than sink so low.

Some time after, I was going through the ashtrays of my acquaintance. I always had a rich harvest at my friend Liebezahl's, who often hosted black marketeers with lavish smoking habits. Johanna needed her own ends, and my landlady Frau Stabhorn counted the ends of her smoking visitors and could cut up rough if she noticed there was one missing. To be fair, I will say that she occasionally let me have the odd one of hers.

In a busy street one day, I saw an elderly man creep round a parked car, bend down, and pick a sodden end out of the gutter. Good grief, I thought, I may have come down a little in the world, but you'll not catch me doing that.

An hour later, I was standing at a bus stop when a Belgian gentleman threw away a cigarette end. And what an end it was! My heart stopped when I saw it lying in the dirt, all white and fat, and just about the length of a baby's finger. If I'd hesitated for a second, a greedy-looking youth would have beaten me to it.

So I never even noticed that one day there was no smoker in the world so degenerate that I could look down on him. I stood so low that no one could stand below me.

And then just the other day, I threw away a cigarette end, and since then I've thrown away many more. And now I get to my feet and enjoy the experience of taking an overflowing ashtray and emptying the contents out in the lavatory.

When I return with the emptied ashtray, I find Heinrich in intense conversation with Luise and Johanna. "I could never marry an uncultivated man whom I viewed as an inferior," says Luise.

"What do you mean by inferior?" asks Johanna. "What do I care if someone isn't my social equal and is uncultivated from the point of view of a university professor?"

Luise assumes an arrogant expression. "You don't even believe that—would you take a sewage worker or a garbageman?"

Johanna dangles her legs over the chair arm and laughs. "Why not? If he's nice, and I fancy him! I want someone for me, not for other people. Sooner a garbageman who's a good husband to me than a senator who bores me and is a rotten husband."

Just as well that Heinrich is cultivated and is a prospect for Luise. I could have brought Habermann too, I suppose. Habermann is interested in Luise, and I've always taken care to foster that interest.

Before the currency reform Habermann used to supply cauliflowers, leeks, and potatoes to the Klattes (for my sake) and was always respected and flattered for doing so by them. He was treated not just as a social equal but as a superior and a benefactor. Frau Klatte would put out cushions for him to sit on, Herr Klatte would humbly and gratefully fill his pipe from Habermann's tobacco pouch, and Luise would save clippings for him from the magazines *Farmers' Weekly* and *Allotments and More*. It didn't matter if Habermann dirtied the carpet, his grimy fingernails were eyed with benevolence, and his views were respectfully solicited on such subjects as economic policy, foreign trade, party political programs, nuclear war, and the prospects for the nation. A scholar whom the Klattes had formerly been proud to know was cut dead after he'd once approached Habermann at the Klattes' and got a few pounds of cherries and onions from him. "Hunger makes certain individuals calculating and shameless" were Frau Klatte's words at the time, half-pitying, half-contemptuous.

Habermann was a jealously tended favorite, and I thought I could allow myself the greatest hopes.

I've known him for a long time. He is a man with a heart of gold, a man of whom it is plausibly said that he would worship the ground his wife treads on.

Following the currency reform, though, there were vegetables in profusion, and Habermann became an insignificant and inferior individual where the Klattes were concerned. His good nature and sterling husbandly qualities were disregarded. His father is a night watchman, and he himself a common or garden gardener.

Please God Luise finally sees my social inferiority.
I'm not a cultivated man. My two or three semesters of
German really don't count. I have a brother who is currently a hotel porter in Brazil, another is an agricultural
laborer in the South of France. On the negative side,
I'm sorry to say my mother married a botany professor, while my sister Elfriede is a minister's wife. I have
several relatives who are even more exalted than that, as
well as a whole bunch of others who aren't at all exalted.
They more or less cancel one another out.

Herr Klatte is dancing with one of the Perlbaums and
singing "Life is for living." The other Perlbaum is talking
about varicose veins with Frau Klatte. A liqueur glass has
fallen over. Luise is plucking an imaginary thread off my
sleeve. Women always do that when they want to indicate
ownership of a man. Johanna is stifling a yawn, and she
has runs in her nylons. There was a time when German
women believed nylons lasted forever. Unfortunately,
stocking manufacturers are not altruistic. It is not in
their interests to produce indestructible products.

A glutinous tiredness settles over the company.
When I give the signal for departure, everyone perks up
one last time.

Heinrich kisses the hands of both the Klatte ladies. I
am glad to see that. His eyes are a little glazed over.

Johanna is singing out in the landing. She is such a
good girl, trying to the last to make a bad impression.

Luise drags me into a corner of the hallway. "I know I must never leave you, Ferdi," she says, even though I have asked her hundreds of times not to call me that. "Ferdi, you need someone who will look after you, and make sure you don't go downhill. Imagine what would become of you if you fell in with a slut like that Johanna. I could see she had her beady eye on you. Your friend Heinrich is nice enough, but he doesn't need a wife to keep him up."

So everything turns out differently from the way I hoped.

On the street I pass the Perlbaum girls, who are cheerfully pushing their empty handcart in front of them. If I have the chance I'll pinch an iron from my mother-in-law and slip it to those good girls to make up for the bombproof door and window frame.

On the corner, I run into Heinrich and Johanna. It's a good feeling to have escaped this forced conviviality. I feel like drinking a cup of coffee with them and lapsing into an easy, harmonious tiredness together. Perhaps we'll go up to Johanna's for half an hour.

"Do you mind if I walk your cousin home?" asks Heinrich. "I do really like your fiancée, in terms of my readership profile she's extremely interesting to me. It probably wouldn't occur to your cousin here to read a solid family journal, but then I'd quite like to stop thinking about work for five minutes." Before I can say anything, they both steer for a taxi. And there I was, thinking they liked me and valued my company.

A soft damp mist puffs up out of the ruins. There's a smell of earth. Slowly I traipse along the unlit street to my cold bed at the Widow Stabhorn's.

My mother Laura

Laura is coming. Laura is my
mother. Ever since I can remember, we children called her Laura.
It's a round sort of name, and one
that suits her. It almost doesn't
feel like a name to me anymore.
If I ever had another mother, I
would call her Laura as well.

Laura is big and stout. My father, we children. and all our friends would have been sad if Laura had ever lost a pound of her majestic, soothing fat. We were all fortified by our belief in Laura's immutability.

Laura has delicate joints and small hands and feet. She has a beautiful, calm face and dark, lustrous straight hair. Laura would never have had her hair marcelled or waved. It's not in her nature to take measures.

The most beautiful aspects of Laura are her eyes and her voice. She has very large eyes that look like pools of dark golden varnish, and heavy lids with long lashes. Usually these eyes are half-closed, and it's a great surprise whenever she decides to open them wide. Her voice is soft and purring and unexcited.

I can't remember ever having seen her agitated or cross. Laura is a genius of sleep. She loves to spend her life, as much as possible, recumbent. As soon as some embarrassment, annoyance, or problem is brought to her, Laura goes to sleep, breathing calmly, with a serene smile.

Laura is lazy. Many women are justly praised for their industry. The thought of Laura industrious would be frightful indeed if it weren't frankly impossible.

It's possible that I owe my life to Laura's indolence. I am convinced that it's chiefly out of indolence that Laura had one child after another. I have four brothers and three sisters, not including half-siblings. In any case, I owe my charmed infancy to Laura's indolence.

Laura was eighteen when she married my father. For any other woman, my father would have been the most difficult husband imaginable. He was unable to ruffle Laura's calm. He needed her the way the vineyard needs the sun. My parents' marriage was unusual but happy.

My father was a painter. He was known in his time, maybe he will one day become famous. He was crazy about painting, really obsessed with it. It killed him that he wasn't a second Rembrandt. Laura let him rage and wail. Most women are inclined to soothe their husbands at great length, when soothing is the last thing they need.

Our income, as you might imagine, was irregular. In her dealings with creditors and bailiffs, Laura manifested antique greatness. A colleague of my father's was once heard to say that with a wife like that it must be a pleasure for a man to have debts.

I can remember one bailiff in Munich who made the most hard-boiled debtors tremble. Not Laura. "Markus," she said softly and slowly to my father, "they can't lock us up or take our children away, and they're not allowed to beat us or cut up your painting, so why don't you just go up to your studio."

"Your calm drives me wild," my father yelled back. Laura closed her eyes and, smiling, fell asleep.

She received the bailiff lying on the sofa. We children were formed up into a picturesque group on the hearthrug. The bailiff said, oh, I don't know, something or other. With a charming smile my three-year-old sister Nina offered him a sweet. Laura batted her eyelids open and said mildly, "We would have liked to give you something as well"—I can remember the bailiff retreating in polite confusion after that.

A landlord in Stuttgart was not so gentle. The approach he tried was crude. "Come back when you've calmed down a little," Laura said and irrevocably went to sleep.

In Berlin one day my brother Toni's teacher turned up at Laura's. He was in a terrible state because he had something awful to say to her. Finally, he managed to spit it out: he had caught Toni telling lies, and not just once. "Lord," said Laura, "we all have to lie on occasion, and Toni I'm sure will do too, so he might as well get some practice at it now. I hope he's got a good memory; perhaps you should make sure he knows when he's lying because otherwise it's easy to get confused." The teacher looked baffled; Laura ended the interview by falling asleep.

My father would fall in love from time to time. We lived with it the way that in other families they lived with the father having allergies. As long as the girl or woman in question staved him off, my father would be difficult and tense. His work suffered. Since the objects of passion were usually regular visitors, we were all at pains to wrap them in cotton wool and charm them. When my father got his way, the whole family for a few days would experience cloudless happiness. We had the most delightful nannies who felt terrible towards Laura and tried desperately and in all sorts of ways to make themselves pleasant and useful in the household. Some of them stuck around long after my father had deserted them. As soon as his passion had ebbed away, the abandoned creature was given into Laura's care. There were periods during which Laura had three or four girls in her care. We got to see the agreeable side of them, cooking, cleaning, knitting, and lamenting the fickleness of men in general and in particular.

Laura kept a feeling of honest gratitude towards the girls. When a lady once intimated to her that her husband had never been unfaithful to her, Laura said without the least irony, "Oh, you poor thing, how can you stand it?"

Often father's brother, Uncle Kuno, would help out. He was a solid man who could hang on to his money. He never got around to marrying because he was so completely absorbed by our family.

Sometimes there was only enough lunch for three people, and then Laura would farm us out to other families. "I don't want my children to starve," she would declare, and send us each somewhere else. "Stay there

whether they want you or not, make yourselves agreeable
and tell them someone's collecting you in the evening."

Occasionally, it would transpire that some of us
would spend several weeks or months with relatives
or acquaintances in the country or abroad. Usually the
other families would try and give us a strict upbringing,
and we were always happy to be back with Laura, where
we weren't threatened with any pedagogical measures.
I was keenly envied by my classmates at school because
my mother would sign the most horrifying report card
without even looking at it. Once I appeared with seven
other small boys, who all wanted Laura to sign theirs for
them. Laura was sorry she couldn't oblige. "I twice had
to repeat classes and my marks were always terrible, especially in conduct," she told the fascinated lads. Laura
was incredibly popular with my friends and the friends
of my siblings. Her room was often full of children, like
a youth protest. The children didn't bother her. When
she had enough of them, she went to sleep. The wildest
din wasn't enough to keep her awake.

When I was ten, my father died of a lung infection. I
happened to be staying with a great-aunt in Amsterdam,
so I don't know if Laura cried. I think, at the deepest
level of her being, she went on living with him.

Uncle Kuno took over the management of the household. He moved the whole family to Bonn, where he had
a chair in botany.

He was very lucky that we boys had innate housewifely talents. Leberecht had a swift and charming
way of laying the table and an inspired technique for
washing up. At the age of thirteen, Matthäus attached
buttons for the whole family, and could bake bread
and cake. My fourteen-year-old brother Luitpold and
I had mastered electrical appliances, could run the
coal-burning stove perfectly, and bottled fruit and vegetables. By the time I was eleven I outperformed Luitpold
in this last discipline, and during bottling season was
loaned out to sympathetic families to whom we felt in-
debted. Toni cleaned windows, made beds, and invented
vegetarian dishes that no one liked. He had read a book
about the meat trade in Chicago that had turned him off
meat. He was crazy about animals. In Toni's presence, no
one would have dared squash a bug.

Unlike us boys, the girls were perfectly useless in
the household. Before little Nina could walk, she used to
crawl around in Father's studio. She could draw before
she could write. In Bonn she practically died from missing him so. Apart from crying, drawing, and painting,
there was nothing she could do.

Aloisia was fifteen at the time and already so beautiful that she had no other occupation than to allow
herself to be stared at adoringly and delightedly by the
family. "Come here, Aloisia, I want to look at you for five
minutes," said Laura, and Aloisia let herself be looked

at. "Thank you, Aloisia," said Laura, before she went to sleep.

Oh, how Laura enjoyed her sleep. She lived in it, it made her happy. I wonder: does she still have such strong and joyful sleep? Laura mustn't change.

It was Laura who made it possible for Aloisia to accept her beauty the way a bird might accept its ability to fly. It doesn't suffer from it, it's not proud of it. We all accepted ourselves with our gifts and our shortcomings, remote from any wish for change.

Once, when I was once bottling greengages with Luitpold, I suddenly felt a slicing yearning for my father, his thin ash-blond hair, his venerable pipe, his irascibility and absentmindedness. I longed for his violent tenderness and was gripped by the sort of mute perplexity I sometimes saw him in. I crushed a large round greengage in my hand and felt the corners of my mouth quiver. Luitpold looked at me. "He drew a squirrel for me once," he said. "Let's both cry." We cried for a few minutes, and then we went back to bottling greengages.

We drew a distinction between quasi relatives and real relatives. Uncle Kuno was a real relative. He had Father's soft hair, his nursery blue eyes, and his broad rumpled brow. You only realized how different he was from Father after you'd noticed how similar he was.

"What made you give the children their names, Laura?" Uncle Kuno asked once. "Nina, Toni,

Ferdinand—they're just about all right. But why Aloisia and Leberecht?"

We got our names from the respective officials to whom our father reported our births. Other parents spend months racking their brains as to what name to give their little darlings *in spe*. They spend days and nights working on a name that they might have come upon in half an hour. My parents exercised themselves as little as possible over their future darlings; they gave themselves time till they were there. Each new birth would plunge my father into a sea of guilt and made him prepared to offer Laura any conceivable sacrifice, even the walk to the registrar's office. Officialdom affected him the way some women are affected by mice; even getting him to buy a stamp at a post office counter was torture. I inherited this morbid trait of his.

"Remind me, what are we calling him, Laura?" he would ask hurriedly as he was leaving the house. He was anxious to have the torment behind him and be back home with her. Laura suggested names she happened to think of. "Why not something different for a change, Markus? I'm thinking Lisbon, Coco, Mazurka, Pampas, New Moon."

My father was all ready to fulfill her wish. But by the time he was at the registrar's, either he had forgotten her suggestions or else the official's reaction was frosty and disdainful. He suggested names to Father that he liked, and Father straightaway gratefully agreed, just so he could get away from the oppressive atmosphere as quickly as possible. Once back home, he would have forgotten again. It was sometimes weeks before someone took the necessary research upon himself and the family learned the name of their newest addition.

Today I am quite glad I am not called New Moon or Tobacco. An unconventional name is nothing but trouble.

My sister Elfriede, the minister's wife, was always an alien in our family. She continually criticized us and did all she could to try and improve us. Even today she likes to appear good and noble. There may be something laudable about such an ambition, but since people usually strive to be or to seem what they are not, it tends to provoke suspicion and unease. When Laura heard Elfriede's footfall, she straightaway fell asleep.

Even physically, Elfriede was unlike the rest of us. We were all dark, nimble, and sinewy as squirrels. Elfriede was lardy, Gouda blond, and slothful. Perhaps she was swapped as a baby. A mother other than Laura would probably have checked, but it's not in Laura's nature to take any unnecessary steps. She is not one of those women who, when offered something by a shopkeeper, asks, And is it fresh? Laura understands there are no shopkeepers who would say, Actually, no, it's stale.

Similarly, no maternity unit would admit that they make mistakes over the labeling of babies. And of course, Laura has so many of her own children that she can quite easily accommodate a stray.

Elfriede generally felt happiest when staying with those relatives the rest of us liked least. I was once put with her in the house of three great-aunts. I was afraid of them because they made it their business to give me an upbringing, and for all their efforts, I continued to do everything all wrong. Elfriede had no trouble at all, she was exemplary in every way, and continually about some charitable good works. At school she was the one who pinned up the maps, dragged the stuffed animals into the room for art class, and carried the form mistress's books.

I was nine years old when for the first and only time in my life, the possession of a sum of money drove me to despair, because I was unable to spend it.

Elfriede and I had brought our piggy banks with us from home. My piggy bank contained a lot of coppers, but also a twenty-mark note folded up small that a generous uncle had given me because I had asked for an airplane for Christmas.

When our piggy banks were full, to my chagrin they were taken away from us by our aunts, so that we could buy something useful with them later.

I saw myself faced with the perverse obligation of having to steal my own money. Secretly, with a hairpin, I managed to fiddle the twenty-mark note out of the piggy bank.

That afternoon, I persuaded Elfriede to come out and spend the money with me. I wasn't completely convinced of her trustworthiness, but our common exile had brought her closer to me and I relaxed my vigilance towards her. A vague instinct told me not to confess my grand auto theft, and I told her a preposterous story about a school inspector who had driven up in a glass coach and given me the money. I was told to spend it with my sister. It was foolish of me to allow Elfriede to take part in my adventure. Perhaps I thought it made me more secure if I had her participation. Perhaps, conversely, it was the added danger of including her. Perhaps I was driven by a devil to entangle this perennial good girl in a web of sin and drag the lofty creature down into the mire. Perhaps I only took Elfriede because there were no other children on hand.

Elfriede was a year older than me, but the possession of the twenty marks briefly gave me seniority.

First, I led her to a lemonade stand, where there were bottles of red, yellow, and green drinks. We sampled them all. Elfriede's moral resistance was broken, and my sense of enterprise drew her with me.

The seals on these soda bottles were round balls of glass. I had often made the attempt to remove one from its bottle. There was nothing I desired more than one of these glass balls. In my lemonade intoxication I bought an extra bottle to take with us. With thumping heart and the feeling of a murderer disposing of a body, I smashed the bottle against the curb. At last I was left with the glass ball in my fingers. I no longer know what miracle I hoped for from its possession. Probably none. The little ball was enough of a miracle. I had freed it from its glass prison, and violently done to death a glass body for its sake. It had cost me some resistance, because everything was alive where I was concerned. I thought I hurt a sheet of paper if I tore it in half.

The magic of the ball was joined by the magic of money. I had feared my twenty marks wouldn't be enough for the orgy at the lemonade stand. I had poked it nervously in the direction of the lemonade man, only to be given an overwhelming mass of notes and coins in change.

I went with Elfriede to an ice cream van. We were living high on the hog and knew no restraint. How many times I had dreamed of eating all the ice cream I wanted. Elfriede even outdid me in her performance. She ate stolidly and knew neither distraction nor excitement.

I paid with a note and was given change. Once again, my money had increased. I bought licorice sticks, rasp-berry drops, twenty gummy bears, and rolls of mints. My money knew no diminishment. On the contrary. My trouser pockets were bursting with small coins. Elfriede was getting floppy and teary, and I had the grim feeling I was cursed.

On a fairground, Elfriede and I found a carousel. After five rides, Elfriede promptly vomited. She wanted to go home. That wasn't possible. First, the money had to be gone. I saw no possibility of hiding it at home. Discreetly I tried to lose a few coins. Elfriede noticed, and retrieved them in spite of her poor condition. "It's wrong to throw away money," she justly inveighed, "let's give it to the aunts." I wasn't happy with that. Desperately, I thought how I could get through the remaining money. Nothing came to mind. I must have had an inadequate imagination, and what I did have was lamed by Elfriede's presence. If I'd had proper, legitimate access to the money, I might have bought myself goldfish, roller skates, tortoises, or a canary. But as it was, these things were all impossible.

I proposed giving the money to a beggar. At that time there were beggars everywhere. But now that I was looking for one, I couldn't find one. For half an hour I dragged Elfriede through the town on a vain search.

I thought about going into a café, but didn't dare, for fear of maybe being arrested. I bought ten packets of burnt almonds from an automat. Those ten coins didn't seem to weigh much. Besides, I was now obliged to choke down a whole heap of burnt almonds. Elfriede offered little by way of support. We should have been home long ago. Our lateness meant we were in for the third degree.

I toyed with the notion of burying my awful riches under a tree, but there was no suitable tree and I had no shovel. Elfriede wouldn't allow me to drop the money in a deserted passageway or letterbox somewhere. I obeyed her, because I still hoped she would stay mum when we got home.

As a last resort, I thought I would give the money to the greengrocer woman in our street. I didn't have any feeling that I was doing the woman a kindness. I just thought she might take the curse off me, because she'd always been nice to me in the past.

I emptied my pockets out onto her counter and hurried away with no explanation, feeling guilty. Outside, Elfriede was just choking on a burnt almond which she had accidentally gulped down unchewed.

Half an hour later, and Elfriede had given our aunts a flawless account of my crimes—at least those that were known to her—and spilled tears of remorse for her own culpable involvement in them. Since I was no longer in a position to tell what was true and what was a lie, I said nothing. My great-aunts seemed not to believe the story of the school inspector in the glass coach.

In the end, the greengrocer woman turned up, asking what she was supposed to supply in return for the money that I had left with her. She assumed I had come to her on the instruction of my aunts.

Too late it occurred to me that I could have used the money to buy myself a ticket home to Laura.

Money never forgave me for my offensive behavior. It has avoided me and still to this day claims not to know me. I never again had too much of it, and very often not enough. And that's not always pleasant.

Money is more demanding than the most demanding mistress. It doesn't like to be treated as the means to an end, it wants to be loved for itself, it demands loyalty and devotion, otherwise it will up and leave.

Love, even love of money, demands talent. I will never come to money. I must reconcile myself to the fact, just as I must reconcile myself to the fact that I can't bite through a horseshoe, compose Beethoven's Ninth, or perform brain surgery.

A year after my father's death, Laura married Uncle Kuno. It would have been bothersome for Laura to wait for some stranger. Uncle Kuno loved Laura, and he was stuck with our family as it was. Uncle Kuno doesn't exactly have the makings of a millionaire, but unlike my father he knows how to deal with money.

I always made a bad impression when I said I never had the orientation towards any particular trade or profession. I might have liked to be a rodeo rider, but unfortunately I didn't have the qualifications.

I have no aptitude for business. I don't think I could even go bankrupt successfully. As an official I'd be about as much use as a brick playing a bouillon cube. Occasionally I am left speechless with admiration for those individuals who go to an office every morning to spend eight hours there doing something that leaves them as figures of horror to their fellow humans.

Nor do I feel drawn to any of the punitive professions. Among these I would include customs and excise officials, detectives, bailiffs, various types of comptroller, tax inspectors, electricity account managers, dogcatchers, policemen in red-light districts. I'm sure all these are necessary, honorable, and deserving professions. It's just that I don't have the degree of moral determination to exercise a profession whose essence is the continual persecution of a certain well-defined portion of the population. I can't imagine closing a bar humming with joie de vivre just because last orders have come and gone, or, as a customs inspector, pulling a contraband diamond from the ear of a nice lady. I don't want to cuff anyone or disconnect their gas. The afflicted parties always make such a helpless tragic impression.

Nor am I any better suited for the academic professions. Physics and chemistry are bottomless mysteries where I am concerned. The law is depressing. If I were a schoolteacher I would bring children up the wrong way (away from the generality) and as a doctor I would show my patients that I had no confidence in my diagnoses.

It would be a simple matter if you could just do a job you knew you could do. For instance, I'm a good electrician, though I have no professional training. I have done lots of things in the course of my life, usually without official sanction.

Among other things I've been a pub chef, a tailor, car mechanic, actor and prompter in a traveling theater group, swimming teacher, ice-cream salesman, long-distance lorry driver, gardener's assistant. I can sew and darn, wash and iron clothes, speak several languages fluently and wrong, design rock gardens, resole shoes, fix broken wireless sets, wave ladies' hair, milk cows, repair fishing nets, breed canaries, and drive more or less anything, from a bus to a motor launch. It's amazing how many aptitudes a man can find in himself if given time to think. I don't suppose I'll ever really be on my uppers. Brazenness has got a lot going for it.

My happiest time was as a bookseller in the old center of Cologne.

My brother Luitpold was studying law, and I was studying German. We were both studying to humor Uncle Kuno. Today Luitpold has a small carpentry business in Sigmaringen and is happily married to Lucca the Flying Fish, a former trapeze artiste.

I was really only studying on the side; my main occupation was working as a car mechanic. Medieval German wasn't going to help me with the demands of the modern era, and knowledge of the Merseburg charms probably wouldn't get me a piece of bread anywhere at all. An accumulation of specialisms is a luxury a man can only afford under quite specific financial conditions.

I had a friend who was crazy about Chinese porcelain. Put him in a social gathering and he would talk for hours about the Ming dynasty, and was respected as a highly cultivated fellow. Then once he ran out of money, people turned away in boredom the moment he opened his mouth, all except for a vegetable seller in the market who was three parts deaf and in better days had been going out with my friend's erstwhile cook. His knowledge of all those Mings wasn't even enough to get him a hot lunch or a marriage to a well-situated elderly widow. For women who have their own pad and a solid income there's no such thing as a shortage of men. Now my Ming friend is leading a sorry existence as a salesman in a tacky antique shop, and he suffers from low self-esteem because he is unable to make use of his valuable knowledge.

At the time we were both students, it was Luitpold who was the first to befriend Uncle Hollerbach. Uncle Hollerbach owned a bookshop with a philately section in the old town of Cologne. The entire building that housed it wasn't much bigger than a birdcage, and the shop window was the size of a hand towel. That anyone could

actually live from what this hidden mini-enterprise
threw off sometimes appeared to me as a biblical miracle. But then there are a lot of people of whom I am quite
unable to say whether and how they live. Sometimes I
don't even understand myself.

My brother Toni always maintained that people who
work hard contribute to their own impoverishment. If
his theory is correct, that might explain Uncle Hollerbach's comparative wealth. Because he wasn't a hard
worker; he drank.

At the same time every afternoon he calmly shut
up shop and walked with firm purposeful stride to a
dingy, thinly visited pub on the corner. There he would
sit on the same wooden bench at the same wobbly table
and was served by the same colorless waiter. Silently
the waiter would bring him a glass of gin, silently Uncle
Hollerbach took it. Between his seventh and eighth gins,
Uncle Hollerbach would drink a beer against the thirst,
this too brought him by the silent waiter. Even after fifteen gins Uncle Hollerbach was no more loquacious. His
posture was upright and alert, his movements few and
calm. Why did he drink, if not to change? Everyone who
drinks does so to change himself or his outlook, which
comes to the same thing. What was going on in Uncle
Hollerbach?

I got to know Uncle Hollerbach through Luitpold.
He was Luitpold's discovery. Uncle Hollerbach was no

misanthrope, he liked to have someone sit with him silently keeping pace with him. Luitpold is a mild-mannered and cooperative person with a sense of the requirements of other souls. He was and still is a good drinker. Unfortunately, he has one quirk. Quirks are things that take getting used to by others, and that mustn't be sprung on them. Otherwise, it is possible for someone with a quirk to affect others like an earthquake.

Luitpold was always quiet and reticent. If there was drinking to be done, he helped to do it. He happily carried drunks from bar to bar or bar to home. He had the innocent strength of a gorilla. In a drinking situation, he seemed like a monument to peace. He didn't sing, he didn't row, he was never overtaken by some urgent communicativeness or lachrymose sentimentality, he didn't start telling off-color jokes or pester ladies with his bibulous adhesiveness. The more astonishing, then, this particular quirk. When, unnoticed by those around him, he had reached a specific degree of intoxication, he swiftly and silently removed all his clothes. No matter where he was—on the street, at home, in a professor's sitting room, on the terrace of a wine bar or in a poky pub. As soon as someone told him to get dressed, he would look sad, but obey. The following day he suffered agonies of remorse and found his behavior so monstrous and unlike himself that he was unshakably convinced

such a thing would never happen to him again, whereupon he serenely sought out the danger at the next
opportunity.

He had been out drinking three times with Uncle
Hollerbach in cordial silence without this quirk having
overtaken him. He had kept up with Uncle Hollerbach
and was on the way to drinking himself into the other
man's affections. The fourth time, a slight inner imbal-
ance had lowered his resistance to alcohol, and then, as
through autohypnosis, he had started to strip. He had
forced Uncle to abandon his noble silence and display
a vulgar chattiness. "Get dressed," Uncle had said, and
got the colorless waiter to order a taxi. He had had to go
looking for a missing shoe of Luitpold's, had left the
pub ten minutes earlier than usual, and was four gins
short of his quantum. All these details were brought
to my attention later by the colorless waiter, who, while
happy to serve Uncle in silence, preferred as a rule to
make use of his God-given gift of speech. Luitpold had
just the merest notion of having stripped and so ravaged
and disgraced Uncle's carefully ordered life. Luitpold's
morning-after moods could reach a pitch where he
would allow himself to be put to death as a serial killer
with the feeling it was no more than he deserved. The
courage to beard Uncle once more could only have come
to him in that same state of unconscious drunkenness
that had the inappropriate consequences.

Of course, I find Luitpold exaggerated in his sense of his excesses. But the man has a tender nature and is a shy, reticent individual, and that can't be changed. It was with great trouble I kept him from going to a psychoanalyst to have his quirk investigated. A professional would have felt it incumbent upon himself to turn up such deep psychic chasms in Luitpold that my poor brother would never have recovered. I think at worst Luitpold will be a subconscious sun-worshipper, or he will have felt an irresistible urge to go to bed, regardless of time and place. If one let him be, one would probably find him with hands folded sitting on his pile of clothes, mumbling a child's prayer before lapsing into gentle slumber.

Luitpold begged me to go to Uncle Hollerbach and see if he had perhaps had the pub torn down and dropped in the Rhine piece by piece. There are ways he is inclined to overestimate himself.

But there stood the pub, perfectly intact, where it had always stood, and there sat Uncle Hollerbach, quietly sipping gin in the place Luitpold told me was his. He had a round belly, flyaway grey hair, and a large red face with a Caesar nose, a resolute chin, bushy eyebrows, and a mariner's twinkling blue eyes. In introducing myself, I wasn't entirely able to avoid the medium of speech. With a gesture of welcome he had me sit down, and with a light majestic nod ordered me a glass of gin.

From that day forth I was Uncle Hollerbach's drinking companion. I have no oddities, drunk or sober. When drunk, I adjust to my surroundings. If there is singing, I sing along. If a pretty girl indicates she might like to be embraced, I embrace her. If a party feels called upon to reveal the ultimate mysteries of life in the course of sweeping philosophical discussions, I reveal too. If someone can do nothing but bewail his misery and the misery of the world, I have tears set aside for that purpose. My personality does not seek to dominate. At the most, I might manage to withdraw from a context if it displeases me.

At first, I tried to assert myself in Uncle Hollerbach's presence by speaking. I interpreted his sparse sign language as encouragement, while his blue gaze directed at me indicated that I had his attention. From the quivering of his brows, a slight pushing forth of his lower lip I inferred agreement and replies. I told him about my fellow students and my studies, of the fair and unfair treatment I got from the mechanic, of uncouth customers and my charming punctilious way of dealing with them. I talked with wisdom and resignation about the political situation and intimated that I was probably the only man alive who could see and understand it all. I spoke illuminatingly about Dante, Dostoevsky, Gide, and Tolstoy. I held forth on the prostitution of the fourth estate and the vanity and selfishness of our leading politicians. I showed myself to be the man who first understood that passion for a woman doesn't last. That striving for political power is not the same as love of the people. That the earth is so despoiled that the moon might as well fall on top of it and squash it flat.

There was more, and I didn't scruple to say it. I spoke up for murderers, check forgers, pimps, landscape painters, sadists, stamp collectors, pacifists, materialists, race fixers, freestyle wrestlers, cannibals, vegetarians, naked dancers, allotment gardeners, Muslims, Calvinists, sybarites, hermits, anarchists. I defended everything that was under attack and laid into everything that to my mind got a free pass. I understood everything and forgave nothing, because I had nothing to forgive, since no freestyle wrestler, pacifist, sadist, hermit, vegetarian, or anyone else had done the least thing to harm me.

Gradually the torrent of my speech dwindled into a river, my river of speech into a brook, my brook of speech into a trickle. And finally, one evening, that trickle ceased, my tongue was dry, and my spirit gave in to a need for thought. It dawned on me that I had said nothing that was really worth saying, that I had talked for the sake of talking, and that my speech had been nothing but foolishness. I had strutted like a peacock before Uncle Hollerbach, all the while supposing I'd been showing him the rare insights of an exceptional intellect. Uncle's stony silence had prevailed. I too was silent, without forcing myself and without boring myself. I saw that the words of the brain are not like the words of the mouth. My ideas had tumbled out of me like unripe fruit. Now I accorded them some quiet and time to recover, during the hours I passed with Uncle Hollerbach.

From the very first moment, I had felt drawn to Uncle. I found him more mysterious and alluring than any woman. At that time almost any female would draw my eye, but I was far more curious about Uncle Hollerbach. What was going on in him? Was anything? Or was he just living in dullness? Was he happy or unhappy? Why did he drink? Was there anything in this world that he loved? What tied him to life? Was he good? Did he have it in him to be bad? Was he wise or foolish? Had he had rare spiritual experiences? What was he like as a child? Could he remember anything? What can one learn from a person who doesn't speak? To me speech was the only conduit between one person and another. Well, now I saw that there were many other ways of communication. For the thing that Uncle Hollerbach wished to communicate, he didn't need words.

Even during the time of my loquaciousness I hadn't dared ask Uncle Hollerbach any questions, in spite of my burning curiosity. After he had vanquished me with his silence, I gradually lost my curiosity, even as Uncle Hollerbach lost none of his magic. I took him as he was and felt at peace. It was a new and wonderful experience for me to be with a person I wanted nothing from and who didn't make me want anything either. Most people, myself included, want others to want something of them, regardless of whether they want to give anything or not. One is supposed to turn to them for advice, clever ideas, childhood memories, exclusive confidences, love, absolution of one sort or another, sympathy, all the various services of the heart and brain. They are afraid of being the sort of person people want nothing from. The German language supposes it is being harsh when it says of someone, "I wanted nothing to do with him." Uncle Hollerbach saved me from unthinkingly falling for the expression. He was precisely someone no one wanted anything to do with. He wanted to be that. I wanted nothing from him either. But I was happy in his company and listened happily to the pure sound of our wanting-nothing-to-do-with-one-another.

I was away from Cologne when Uncle Hollerbach died. One day I learned that he had died and that I had inherited his little shop and contents. At the time I was a long-distance lorry driver on the Munich–Berlin route, and I was in love with the wife of a scrap merchant. I can dimly remember she wanted to divorce him because he beat her and that I was somehow titillated by the idea of the delicate blond woman in the middle of so much bulky scrap metal.

I left the scrap merchant's wife without the least compunction and emotionally accepted Uncle Hollerbach's inheritance. I tried to live as Uncle had done, in silence, as a hermit. And yet I forgot the lesson of his lifetime, and I left the poor deceased no peace, but bothered him endlessly, prying into his former life and fitting it out with my fantasies. I barely stopped short of brazenly summoning his voice to spiritualist sessions. I am uncomfortable with belief in the occult, but it is not for me to deny such a thing to the believer. I am mystified where blameless cultivated ladies and gentlemen get the neck to summon the ghosts of the indifferent dead. To summon them! Give Beethoven a table-turning and ask him if the price of potatoes is going up.

If I die before her, I'm sure my fiancée Luise would have me summoned. I can feel the very idea of it making me purple with rage. Even alive, I dislike being summoned by her. Should she dare to do so after my death, I'm sure my spirit would meet her with some earthy invective. Why don't the occultists understand that if that's what they wanted, then spirits would come of their own accord? To my mind, a séance is a display of boorishness, and the more people believe in them, the worse it is. Even the grieving and pining of a loving consort provides scant justification. Who knows if a person in the Beyond even wants to be loved anyway? It's a terrible thing that women like Luise ride roughshod over others' wishes, imagining that the mere fact of loving them gives them all possible rights. Beyond that, many individuals are of the opinion they can make God a little pliant by loving Him with passionate humility and offering Him sacrifices. They never stop to ask themselves whether God is even in the mood for love and sacrifice, and doesn't rather find them a pain in the neck.

I expect the reason the Devil is so frisky is because he isn't being love-bombed the whole time. If only people weren't so convinced that their love was a general blessing. It's a fine thing to love. It's a gift to be allowed to love. If it should come to pass that a human being fills me with love, then I hope I will be able to feel gratitude above all things, whether or not they reciprocate and love me.

I wasn't an occultist and I never summoned Uncle Hollerbach's spirit. But I sensed its presence in the moldy furniture, the dusty shelves, the yellowed books, and the gin bottles that I emptied in memory of the noble departed. I bought three geranium plants and bred carrier pigeons in the little courtyard. It was a gentle life, and especially charming to me because I took it to be a sort of holiday, purely temporary. And it did in effect soon pass.

When I was released from POW camp, it was principally for the sake of the little shop that I made my way to Cologne, even though I knew the shop no longer existed.

I had no other reason to go to Cologne. I had no reason to
go anywhere else either, mind.

I'm not from Cologne, I'm not even from the
Rhineland. If someone asks me, "And where do you
hail from?" I never know how to answer. My mother
was born in Brazil, grew up in Holland, and married in
Germany. My father came from Brandenburg, grew up
in Cologne and Koblenz, studied in France, and later
lived all over the place. And me? I was born in the middle of Lake Constance. I don't like to admit as much,
especially not in any official context, because it makes
such a frivolous impression. Even if well-disposed listeners will understand that I'm not responsible for the
arrangements made by my parents—they do somehow
give me some of the blame. I spent my childhood in ten
cities spread out over three countries. Such feelings
as local patriotism or *campanilismo* never had a chance
with me. At the moment I feel homesick for the South
of France, tomorrow I might have a hankering to be by
the North Sea, and the day after it could be Munich or
Brussels.

Soon Laura will be here. She's still the most anchor-
ing thing in my life. Just now she's in Austria, where
Uncle Kuno has been in charge of a botanical garden for
many years. In the autumn he's going to Bonn to resume
his professorship. That way I'll get to see the city of our

new fairy-tale government princes.* I failed to exercise my ballot this time. I thought all the parties were so outstanding that I couldn't decide to vote for any of them. As a nonvoter I of course represent a horrid antisocial element to all of them, whereas if I'd voted, it could only have been for parties not of my choosing.

Before going on to Bonn, Laura and Uncle Kuno will spend a few days in Cologne. Nina and Aloisia, Toni and Luitpold are coming too. Johanna will throw a huge party for everyone. She loves throwing parties, especially ones that end up involving the police and fire brigade and go down in the memories of those present as unforgettable catastrophes.

My brothers Matthäus and Leberecht won't be there. Mathäus is a farm laborer in the South of France. He is a sun-worshipper. "Germany has no climate," he always says. "God knows what it has instead. For eight months it has a kind of winter, and for four months something that isn't summer." Mathäus is far and away the cleverest of us and probably the one we looked to to make something of his life, in a bourgeois sense. But it so happens he loves the sun and would rather be a beggar under radiant blue skies than a minister-president or millionaire in some cool, foggy country.

---

* In May 1949 Bonn was made the capital of West Germany, ahead of Frankfurt.

Leberecht is no beggar. He has a luxuriant imagination and a strong literary gift. There was a time when he felt under obligation to his talent and turned out novels and stories. Our whole family was excited and lived by his successes. We thought we had finally managed to produce someone with ambition. We encouraged him in any way we could. But one day Leberecht was fed up with writing, and said he'd had it up to here with it. He claimed that writing was the most loathsome profession there was. In order to keep his head above water, he had to write all the time, even when he had no ideas and wasn't in the mood. That was as disgusting to him as having to sleep with a woman he had no feelings for. He could never be anywhere in peace and think about something nice without straightaway being pursued by the feeling he had to put it down on paper and make some money from it. Nor was he stupid and obsessed enough either—unfortunately—to think of his work as something unique and irreplaceable. In a nutshell, Leberecht decided it was better to live an adventure than write one. He was for several years a sailor and is currently a night porter in Brazil.

He is happy and is able to live. My sister Elfriede, the minister's wife, counts him as a disgrace to the family. After the war, the "disgrace" kept his European relatives above water by sending them coffee. Even Elfriede began to view Leberecht as perhaps the most precious of the

Timpe clan. The most celebrated German writer could never have engendered such pride in us as this obscure night porter in distant Brazil. Leberecht's Brazilian life was the only thing that gained me respect and credit with my fiancée Luise, with my parents-in-law, my landlady Frau Stabhorn, and even with my brilliantly successful spiv of a cousin, Magnesius. With ten pounds of coffee before the currency reform I was a highly desirable little nabob of the ruins who would never starve, and who was even in a position to feed others. Those were great, proud days for me, when Leberecht had sent me a package of coffee. I even got sick with emotion and gratitude and had to rest up in bed. But since I knew that Leberecht wasn't a rich man, and always from when he was a boy gave away more than he had, and had others to provide for in addition to me, I wrote to tell him I could get by on my own. Suddenly I didn't like the way almost everyone here had the feeling that people abroad were wallowing in excess and ought to contribute here. Now, following the currency reform, there are endless people who can afford all the coffee, cigarettes, meat, and butter they want. They would be rather stunned to be told by some struggler that they ought to hand over some of their coffee and cigarettes.

I think my brother Toni is the happiest and serenest of us all. Even as a boy, he loved animals and wouldn't eat meat. His vegetarianism remained tolerable even for committed carnivores and didn't turn him into a bigot.

Toni is a gentle creature. Admittedly, like many gentle creatures, he is inclined to be stubborn. He married a mild little wife and owns a flower shop in Starnberg. In his garden he keeps tame squirrels, crows, starlings, rabbits, and bees. I expect he buys honey for the bees and lies down in the sun in summer to feed the mosquitoes, and bakes apple pies for the ravens so they don't eat earthworms. At any rate, I would think Toni's existence is more or less the way he always wanted it to be.

Luitpold is a furniture maker in Sigmaringen. I think he's gone broke five times. In spite of the most alarming circumstances, he's always managed to stay afloat. Luitpold represents the type of good fellow who in nineteenth-century novels gets into trouble by issuing bonds for unreliable friends, allowing bills to fall due, paying allowances to children who were not his, and opening his heart and his wallet to impoverished widows. By the rules of our rough new world he is classified as a noble idiot.

Maybe my sisters, Nina and Aloisia, will come as well.

I am almost a little apprehensive about so much reunion. I hardly dare look forward to it in any pure way. I feel a little embarrassed in advance when I imagine so many possibilities for guilt, suppressed emotion, desperate getting over strangeness. I expect the others will be just as nervous. All except Laura, of course. It's a good thing Laura's coming.

The cheerful adviser

The cheerful adviser is me. Liebezahl has offered me temporary
employment in his swelling
empire. He now has departments
for podiatry, charms, talismans
and scents, departments for
magical cloth, for clairvoyance
and crystallography and the

interpretation of dreams, departments for color, astrology, chiromancy, and graphology.

To help both me and himself, Liebezahl had the idea of extending and supporting his enterprise by taking on a general adviser. Of course, I'm hardly ideal for such a post, but Liebezahl views me as a friend, and he likes to help his friends, inasmuch as economic responsibility will allow. He'd like to give me a run, anyway—at least give me time to buy a coat and a few other necessities. Lord be thanked, it's summer. I don't have to shiver and bless every warm day. I don't like to recall my last coatless winter. Nor do I want to be ostentatiously poor when Laura and the others come. That would be importuning and could compel the good people to charitable acts that might be their undoing. I am already making efforts to eat regular meals so as not to look too hollow-cheeked. I would quite like to earn some money as well, so that I would be able to go away somewhere. I don't know where I would go, and my plans are rather ill-defined, but I'd like to create at least the possibility for myself to travel.

The idea of the cheerful adviser was Johanna's. Liebezahl and I then developed it, after my own initial opposition. It seemed embarrassing to me and not something I could do.

Liebezahl let me have a small whitewashed room with a flame-red carpet and dark-stained oak furniture. At first, he had thought in terms of an Oriental bazaar in which I would be lounging on plump cushions. I would be wearing a burgundy turban and be known as "Camilo, the Font of Eternal Wisdom." In my condition of utter destitution, given appropriate payment, I would have been prepared to stroll about with a scarab in my navel, a leopard skin over my shoulders, and a coffeepot on my head, and to be called "Epaminondas, the Sphinx of the Northern Lights," or anything else for that matter. But in purely technical, business terms I thought the Liebezahl concept ill-conceived. Very well, then let me be a sobersides in a lab coat, playing the headshrinker. I didn't advise that either. Finally, Liebezahl understood that the attention of wide sections of the population was most likely to be engaged by something that approached it in the familiar manner of the advice columns in magazines—something along the lines of "Ask Uncle Baldwin" or "Great-Aunt Adele Gives Advice."

My consultancy comes with an outer office with a secretary and a heap of reference books.

I had no influence on the promotional literature Liebezahl devised for me. According to that, I am a miracle of goodness, patience, experience, neighborliness, empathy, insight, practical common sense, intelligence, and worldly wisdom. I am uncorrupted, modest, cheerful, serious, discreet, instinctive, warmhearted. (These are all the attributes ascribed, as per personal columns, to men or women seeking partners in German family magazines.) And over and above that, I have qualities that no one else has ever had.

Liebezahl bought me a pair of grey flannel trousers and two burgundy sports shirts that I look semi-normal in. He decided against further costumes or uniforms.

So I sit behind my desk, as friendly, ordinary, and confidence-inspiring as possible, and await visitors.

For the first fortnight, things were rather quiet, and I got chiefly clients who were referred to me by the other departments. But this past week I've been kept busy from nine in the morning till eight at night. Gradually I'm getting the hang of it. The very first day I was as nervous as the stand-in who is called upon to deputize for the star in *Othello*. I had no idea what people were going to ask me and what I would reply to them, and at the same time I was being paid for my vast superiority over those poor beings. Instead, I was in such a state that I would ideally have turned to the least of them for advice.

Liebezahl had stashed a bottle of Steinhäger and a roll of mints in my desk drawer. The Steinhäger was to give me confidence, and the mints were to take the alcohol off my breath.

My very first visitor was a woman who wasn't sure whether she should go to Bavaria in October or not. She was looking to me for a decision. Today, questions like hers hold no terrors for me, but at the time I was stumped. The woman didn't give me any lead at all. I

ventured that presumably there would be some fine
autumn weather in Bavaria. She said that wasn't the
point. I said the change would do her good. Luckily, she
agreed with that, but she said it didn't have to be Bavaria. At the end of half an hour I had worked out that
the woman didn't want to go to Bavaria at all, she wanted
to buy primroses. And she didn't really want primroses
either, what she wanted was a midsized pink azalea. It
was like this: her husband's sister was about to cele-
brate her silver wedding anniversary, and they had to
have a present. The woman was in favor of primroses,
because they were the cheapest. The husband thought
a primrose was too cheap. The flower question had led
to marital discord. The woman has a woman friend in
Bavaria whom she would have visited long ago, were it
not that it cost so much to go there. She listed various
things she had acquired in the past few months. Now she
wanted to offer her husband a concession, and buy an
azalea instead of the primrose, because she had thought
how expensive the journey to Bavaria was. And she had
already bought the azalea.

The woman was full of gratitude to me when she left.
I reciprocated. It had taken over half an hour to establish
that the reason she had come was to tell me that she had
bought an azalea.

My next visitor was a tradesman's apprentice who
wanted to get into films and wanted some information

as to which was the most lucrative: actor, screenwriter, or director. I asked my secretary next door for the addresses of some film companies and wished the young man every success; I was sufficiently responsible to tell him as he was leaving not to quit his apprenticeship, it would come in handy whatever he ended up doing.

A fat old lady came in with an imposing shelf of bosom; she confused me by demanding to know whether she should undergo an operation to have her bosom reduced. I showed myself to be a rank amateur in my profession by urging the lady to consult a specialist. When I saw that she disliked my advice, and I started to panic in case she started undressing, I became unusually animated and eloquent. She was wonderfully proportioned; her bosom was absolutely contemporary; men disdained the slim, boyish figure; any number of film stars would count themselves lucky to be possessed of such a bosom, instead of having to mask their inadequacies in celluloid. Yes, and in view of the Goethe anniversary, she should bear in mind that Goethe—our very own Goethe!—was a fanatical advocate and praiser of the female bosom. I thought I had done enough to earn my crust. The lady looked well pleased, it didn't occur to her to leave, and she wanted to hear further hymning of her bosom. She admitted that many men had already spoken as I had, and then she started telling me about these men. Finally, I got her to stop by pointing out that future men were usually more interesting than men in the past, and I referred her to our astrological department.

I am inclined to believe sometimes that people nowadays suffer from shrinkage of the brain. But then I remember that there are still some who don't stream into the Liebezahl conglomerate.

Just now a girl recited a poem she had penned about mummy and tummy and rummy and asked whether she should become an authoress or a film actress. It had also occurred to her to play the football pools. She was a home help, and her chief preoccupation was finding someone to step out with on Sundays. The poor creature was strikingly ill-favored. I suggested a new hairstyle and pressed upon her a few inexpensive changes to her wardrobe. But she didn't want to hear that. So I humored her and said she was so dazzling, most men were probably afraid to approach her; Greta Garbo probably had a similar effect. She, the girl, was in other respects, too, an exceptional creature of uncommon spiritual appeal, and wasted on the average man. I told her to go walking on Sundays and wait till one day she should encounter her exceptional counterpart of the male persuasion. The girl left quickly and happily. Probably to share my verdict on her beauty with some girlfriend.

I have come to the conclusion that most of my female customers haven't come to me for advice at all, but for affirmation of their good points. Others come to dump their emotional garbage and use me as a type of human dustbin.

They have simply fallen victim to the desire to talk about themselves. They can no longer do this with their husbands. Husbands are bad listeners to their wives, being soon bored with accounts of uncanny intuitions, headaches, childhood memories, fascinating emotional complications, observations, and conflicts. Reports of her inner life interest a man only when she's new and he fancies her. To waken the erotic potential of a woman one has to let her speak. Admittedly, what the woman takes to be close attention is often something else, and isn't necessarily directed at what she's saying. Later on, the poor women are surprised and disappointed when the man—so unlike before—has no interest in what his wife once did as an adorable five-year-old tomboy, or how as a teenager one summer her thoughts about bluebells and passing clouds delighted an elderly headmaster and his wife.

During my brief tenure here, I've already learned that it's almost always hopeless to try to enlighten a woman. Not long ago for instance an elderly office worker was telling me how she had a boyfriend three years ago. Then one day he had stopped turning up. He had ignored her letters and tried to avoid seeing her wherever possible. What could possibly be the reason for such behavior? He had told her she was his little darling and he would always love her. So he must still love her.

Should I perhaps tell the woman the plain truth? Someone who doesn't acknowledge a truth under any circumstances won't accept it from others, either. So I told her the man loved her so much he was afraid of being driven mad by it, making him and her both miserable. My explanation made perfect sense to her.

This old office worker is called Fräulein Schwert, and she's become a regular. She doesn't care that the man is threatened with insanity, she wants to see him anyway, even if it does drive him mad. I need to tell her how to win him back. I feel sorry for the old girl, and I wish I could help her, only how? I can hardly truss the man up and mail him to her. I don't believe in medieval potions, nor do I know when, how, and where I am to administer the powdered newt that sat on the head of a white cat during the full moon. I can only wonder where those medieval johnnies got the ingredients for their elaborate potions. Admittedly, I am being forcibly given to understand that parties unhappily in love are capable of anything—except, unfortunately, the conquest of the so passionately desired object of their love.

Sometimes I get the sense that unhappy love is more dangerous than scarlet fever or appendicitis. Fräulein Schwert is a nice person, but she resembles a plucked hen and looks at least a decade older than she is.

I think it's good to enlist the abilities of the unhappy lover. Therefore, I advise Fräulein Schwert to exercise

every morning, to take deep breaths, and brush her hair
for ten minutes, all the while thinking concentratedly
about her Alfred. I have her eat apples, go for walks,
and practice her laugh. The ostensible purpose of all
this is to win Alfred back. Each time I see her, I tell her
she's looking prettier. I think if you tell an unattractive
woman often enough that she's pretty, then it sooner or
later becomes true. Women who never get to hear anything pleasant suffer from a kind of emotional hormone
deficiency. It barely needs saying that the pleasant thing
needs to be said by a man.

There's no point at all in telling an unhappy woman
that she needs distraction. She doesn't want to be distracted. Fräulein Schwert doesn't want to hear about
Thomas Mann, Goethe, the currency devaluation, the
government, the Eastern Zone, or Tito, nor about fat
rations, sunspots, the football pools, Ingrid Bergman, or
Sicilian bandits either. She wants to talk about Alfred.

I seriously wondered what possibilities a girl has to
win a man who no longer wants her. Fräulein Schwert is
by no means my only instance. I get disappointed lovers
in droves. People who write in books and newspapers
that love is dead are unworldly ignoramuses. If they were
to reply that they mean romantic love, then I would say,
yes, but isn't all love romantic? From the days of Adam
and Eve, love between the sexes has remained pretty

much constant. The backdrops may vary, but the feelings themselves don't change.

What did I do myself when my feelings for a girl were over? In most cases, it was the feelings of the girl that were over first, or at any rate soon after. I certainly can't remember a female creature suffering on my account.

I have been doubly attentive of late to my fiancée Luise, since realizing what catastrophic suffering a scorned female heart is sentenced to. I had been well on the way, gradually but certainly coldly and coarsely, to retreating from her. Then, a few days ago, even at the risk of not being able to shake her off in this life, I sent her flowers and chocolates, helped her with their big wash (even though I was dog tired), and almost fell fixing the drainpipe. Luise's grateful smile pierced my heart. I even forced myself to kiss her. I quite understand that I am being woefully inconsistent, but it's more than I can do to consciously make of myself a torturer and a murderer. In my new practice I have witnessed too much in the way of female suffering.

Financial difficulties and work do nothing to diminish Fräulein Schwert's sufferings, either. I don't know whether it's easier for a woman with money or without. People who insist that all sufferings are easier to bear with money might be mistaken. Here, I'm thinking about my customer Frau Meerschuh.

Frau Meerschuh is a well-off young widow who lives alone. Ever since her lover left her, she has been able to devote her entire attention to her broken heart, thanks to her favorable financial situation. Further, having no pressure on her time and money allows her to indulge in pursuits that are turning the man pursued to a hate-filled enemy. She follows him in her car, she bounds up to him in a stream of new garments, she sends him presents and has him spied on by her envoys. It's futile to tell Frau Meerschuh that she should have more self-respect. It's not about self-respect, it's about the man. And it's just as futile to urge her to take up with a grateful and needy homecomer or fugitive from the East.

One can spend hours dinning it into a woman that a man is unworthy of her. She will listen to you and perhaps even agree with you. Then when you heave a sigh of relief and think she's finally seen the light the woman will ask you what she has to do to get him back. Increasingly, I confine myself to listening. Eventually, all feelings come to an end. But woe betide you if you ever say that, because the woman of course doesn't want her feelings to end.

Speaking relieves the pressure on a woman and takes away part of her drive to do something, which left to itself would produce only bad results. The poor things only annoy their friends by permanently going on about some Karl, Gustav, or Alfred. In Liebezahl's institute, they pay their money and are allowed to be annoying.

There's one thing I'd like to press upon all abandoned women: not to lose themselves in fantasies of revenge. After all, there's nothing a man can do about it if his feelings dry up. To have a hundred percent guarantee of not being forsaken, a woman would have to kill her lover during the dog days of his passion. Then she can give herself over to the fantasy that he would have loved her forever, and no one can prove otherwise. Actually or symbolically killing him after he's gone fulfills no useful purpose and would only leave a profound feeling of dissatisfaction.

One Marga Waldweber, an intellectually and physically mature bookseller, has been to see me several times. Only with respect to her Oskar is she weak-willed and frail. She doesn't care about Oskar, let him do what he likes, she's not going to shed a tear for him—only she couldn't understand the manner of his desertion, that was an insoluble puzzle to her. Oskar's passion had withered, Fräulein Waldweber had missed or wanted to miss the indications. She had thought Oskar's love had weakened through business anxieties or a peptic ulcer. It's odd that women's minds are set at ease when a man produces no other love object; business anxieties and peptic ulcers are thought of as harmless. Many a man has returned to an old amour with a new efflorescence of feeling. But many men no longer care to be called sweetie pie, or to kiss the tangled curls and darling hands of a lady and perform the miracles of the Arabian Nights, when they are facing bankruptcy, or an ulcer distracts them from life's sweeter moments. Peptic ulcers and the prospect of bankruptcy are perfectly capable of taking up all a man's attention by themselves.

In a word, Oskar had had enough of Fräulein Waldweber. Nor is he one of those men who like to be comforted or petted. Of course he told Fräulein Waldweber that he still loved her. Few men have the courage to give the wrong answers when women put their notorious leading questions. Certainly, I've never dared tell the truth to a woman who was holding me in her arms. So one day Oskar sent a note to Fräulein Waldweber informing her that they were finished, and he wouldn't see her again. He returned her key by registered parcel in a little box padded with cotton wool. This mode of severance, though, struck Fräulein Waldweber as low and inexplicable. At the very least, Oskar should have spoken to her and returned the key in person. She would like a last meeting. All women want this last meeting. I know that. I have always feared and loathed this last meeting, which is in fact a second-to-last meeting. What on earth is one to say? You say, "It's better this way," and you feel like a heel, because she doesn't at all think it's better this way. You are left with the choice between new deceitful concessions and something that in its disagreeable sharpness outdoes the already accomplished parting. "But what did I ever do to you?" asks the woman, and "You could at least tell me the real reason." She hasn't done anything to you, and if she still doesn't know the real reason, you will never be able to tell her.

Every other day or so, Fräulein Waldweber reappears in a bid to crack the mystery of the returned key. I told her for God's sake not to do anything, and then in a year or so her Oskar would return to her. But she didn't want him back, declared Fräulein Waldweber, it was just on this matter of the key that she wanted to hear from him.

Fräulein Waldweber really believes this. A person who could deceive others the way she deceives herself would be a notorious international crook.

If I can persuade Fräulein Waldweber to put off the conversation regarding the key, then one can assume that after a year at the most her need for Oskar will have vanished. Perhaps it will be time for the next conver- sation with the next man. Many people suffer from a certain recurring illness that affects them at more or less regular intervals. I once heard my friend Dr. Muck telling a female patient of his in serious and dignified German: "It is simply the case with you that this organ is uncommonly susceptible." I was the more impressed because I had no idea what a susceptible organ might be like. Or an organ that was weak and illness-prone.

Well, be that as it may. My lady patients are certainly afflicted. Maybe I should leave them their sufferings instead of trying to cure them. At least suffering is proof of being alive. Can one know how much one diminishes their life by ending their sufferings? The fact that they are attached to their sufferings should give one pause. Sometimes I believe I have helped them. But never yet have I dared to decide if my help was a good thing or not. The only certain help one may offer a person is food if he is hungry, drink if he is thirsty, clothing if he is cold. One can help by reducing his material wants—and perhaps even that only makes him open to fresh emotional wants.

Ever since I have been able to think, nothing has been so repellent to me as the offering of advice to others. Never to do so under any circumstances was among my few principles, yes, I sometimes think it was my only principle. And now I am earning a living by supplying bitter wisdom to poor fools. It's not nice on the part of fate to corrupt me like this, instead of allowing me a modest, ideally inflation-proofed pension. What a plain existence I would then lead, pleasing to the Lord, without ever interfering with any other living being.

My most straightforward cases are the unhappy wives. I don't have to say anything to them, they have come to let off steam about their husbands. It's laudable that they take their complaints to a neutral place. If they talk to their friends and neighbors, they risk filling them with aversion or secret schadenfreude. And if they argue with their husbands, then they will complicate their home lives still further. Most women would rather be married unhappily than not at all. Besides, they are rarely as unhappy as they think they are. Some have an inborn martyr complex and take suffering for a sign of moral superiority. They like to be pitied. For these wives I have a pained frown in the corner of my mouth and a look of melancholy sympathy. That sees me through, and I don't even need to speak. Wives who complain about their husbands have no intention of leaving them. If you're angry, you're not indifferent. A woman who has seriously had enough of her husband and wants a divorce won't waste words and will come to me for the address of a lawyer. Even if she can't leave her husband for financial reasons while she is emotionally detached from him, she will have no interest in talking about him and being pitied on his account.

Now and again, I am sorry that no smart and attractive wives come to me. One hears so much about them. Creatures trembling with hatred and aversion tell me about these evil, sophisticated beings who steal the partners of good, honest women and girls with a grin and a wink. Of course, I esteem the good, honest parties, but over time they pall on me, and I wouldn't mind being refreshed by one of those detestable manstealers. But then I suppose it's hardly ethical to expect payment and to enjoy myself.

Of course, there are also the cheated, abandoned, smitten husbands, but they are a bit of a rarity in my context. They most likely prefer to parade their bleeding hearts to a woman and have them salved and bound by feminine hands. Our graphologist, Ella Kuckuck, is a distinguished expert in emotional injuries in men. She is very striking looking and must be incredibly tough, otherwise she would hardly be able to endure such a procession of sorry, lamenting men day in, day out. Not long ago she told me over lunch that she badly needed a holiday. At the mere sight of a woebegone man she would reflexively begin to yawn. The Samaritan qualities that real women allegedly have in endless supply were on the point of drying up in her.

I can understand Fräulein Kuckuck's feeling of satiety. I wouldn't mind hearing a different tune from time to time. Recently I visited Johanna to experience a change. Her facility was to restore me. I brought along a bottle of cooking brandy that one patient (who suffered from choleric episodes) had stolen from her husband and given me. Less out of love for me than rage at her husband.

Johanna was in tears and greeted me the way a woman would have greeted her rescuer as he plucks her from the lambent flames of her funeral pyre and hoists her onto his sweating, stamping steed. Anton hadn't been seen for five days now. It was like a curse—even in my few hours off, I can't seem to avoid my professional duties.

So of course, as a good professional, I had to listen to Johanna.

Who howled and laid into my brandy and demanded that I restore Anton to her.

Anton is known to me as a somewhat taciturn youth with strikingly sticking-out ears and hands like shovels. Other than that, I never noticed anything especially remarkable about him. Johanna has a way of taking ordinary mortals and transforming them into despotic megalomaniacs. She induces these harmless beings to believe that they are the most desirable creatures under the sun, and the eighth wonder of the world. In some men she develops a gift for exaggeration like no other woman I have ever met. With the possible exception of my sister Aloisia and her apothecary. The main difference is that Aloisia permitted her apothecary to live on in glory to his recent demise, while Johanna suddenly views the apotheosized one as a mortal again and treats him accordingly. She doesn't understand what she's doing with such a man. The man in turn doesn't understand her or the world. Perfectly unscrupulously Johanna lets the toppled one go, into an existence he doesn't understand.

All I can say is, this doesn't seem to have happened to Anton yet.

The case wasn't a hopeless one where she was concerned, since Anton had gone following a scene, and hadn't reappeared. Scenes are no indication of decayed feeling. A scene calls for a reconciliation the way a sausage calls for mustard.

Johanna wanted me to talk to Anton. I was to look for him in his aunt's potato store, grind him to a fine paste, stuff him in my pocket, and leave him on Johanna's not-yet-paid-for twisted-paper carpet. It took considerable experience to make any sense of Johanna's rather unclear demands. Above all, I wanted to know why Anton had made a scene and taken his hat. "There's no reason at all," said Johanna. All right. I tried to find out what reason Anton didn't have. Well, there was Gustav. Who's Gustav? Johanna explained that Gustav was a student. What does Anton have against Gustav's studies? Anton had nothing against Gustav's studies, but Gustav needed books, and he had rheumatism. I thought it was a bit petty to jibe at a fondness for printed matter and rheumatic fever. That led to Johanna mounting an impassioned defense of Anton's character for about the next fifteen minutes. In between she sipped some brandy. She sipped, I sipped. Probably Johanna would now expect me to go to the potato aunt tonight. Whereas I had no intention of going before the day after tomorrow

at the earliest, and I needed to draw strength to lie successfully to Johanna. Displaying the patience of a saint,
I was able to discover from Johanna that the student
Gustav was an old acquaintance and had been sitting in
Johanna's room to borrow some books and rest his rheumatic knee. To relieve his rheumatic arm, he had draped
it around Johanna's shoulder. Anton had walked in, cast
a critical eye on the medical emergency, and grossly
misinterpreted it. Furiously he had slammed the door
behind him. Johanna had come charging out after him,
and Anton had given her a slap and disappeared without
a care for the consequences.

"One should never hit a woman," I said, because
that's what you say to a woman. I did feel pretty indignant. "What a bastard, I'd never hit a woman."

"Of course not," said Johanna, forgetting to cry, "of
course you wouldn't, Ferdinand, you're much too abject
and unemotional." The corners of her mouth dropped
with a leaden display of contempt. "Anyway, what gives
you the right to call Anton a bastard?" Johanna's eyes
bulged with fury. I had barely begun to take in this
phenomenon before Johanna had, with style and power,
slapped my face. I must say, she did make a wonderful-
looking slapper, half radiant Amazonesque triumph,
half sweetly surprised-at-herself femininity. "Oh, I
didn't mean it like that, Ferdinand, did I hurt you?" No,
the slap didn't hurt me. I just felt obliged to book it as

a probable slight, and I wasn't very happy about that. I
don't usually feel so easily slighted. It did incline me
to reconsider Anton's slap, though, and view it mildly,
perhaps even positively.

"Slaps are impulsive acts, and impulsive acts can't
be mean," Johanna lectured me, "I would never hold a
slap against a man, especially one prompted by jealousy.
It's awful if a man is furious about nothing, but indiffer-
ence is always worse."

I was surprised that Johanna hadn't gone to Anton
already and brought him back. Resigned waiting isn't
really her style. Johanna claimed to be scared of Anton's
aunt, having met her once. From her account, the lady
had to be a tigress. I wasn't at all eager to beard such a
creature. Besides, I was distracted by my concerns over
Lenchen.

Lovers are egocentric. It speaks volumes for Johanna
that she is sometimes—love and all—capable of regis-
tering the griefs of others, and even mustering a little
interest in them. "What is it, Ferdinand?" she asked. "I
can tell something's up."

I told Johanna about Lenchen. Lenchen is someone
who came to see me in my office. She has dark shiny
hair, a little white face, and a sad mouth. She seemed
frozen. She wasn't one of the usual seekers after help,
she really needed help. She found it difficult to speak. It
took me time and trouble till she thawed out a little.

Lenchen had just come out of prison, where she had done time for attempted murder or malicious wounding. Her account was not entirely clear, she contradicted herself frequently. After she had begun speaking, I avoided asking her any questions because I was afraid she might fall silent. There are times when the more questions you ask, the fewer answers you get.

Lenchen had had a well-paid secretarial job after the war. Her parents were dead, and her brother gone, along with his estate in East Prussia. Lenchen had a little fourth-floor flat in the city, a bedsitting room and a kitchen. She had met a man who was nice to her, and they had a friendly and peaceful life. One day, a distant cousin by the name of Helga turned up on her doorstep and asked to be taken in for a bit. She came from Berlin and had taken a job in a ladies' outfitters in Cologne. She promised to get a residence permit and a room of her own in a matter of days. The first week, all was affection and harmony. The two girls exchanged confidences over long evening hours. The little room was almost bursting with so many feminine confessions. Lenchen was even pleased when Helga asked if she could stay another week. The third week, she started being less pleased. Her nice boyfriend felt Helga cramping his style, and Lenchen too would have liked some time alone with him. But then she thought that in times like these, lack of charity was twice as bad. Further weeks passed without

Helga moving out. Lenchen started delicately hating the
other woman. The feeling was new to her and alarming;
she had never really hated anyone before. Helga took
over the flat. She helped herself to Lenchen's modest
stock of makeup, her linens, her coffee, her money. She
brought back visitors. She drove away the nice man by
relaying, perfectly innocently, some of Lenchen's confessions. She gave out Lenchen's address as her own. She
went on saying every day that she would leave, but she
never left. She was always suffocatingly sweet and tender. Lenchen waited for Helga to go, stayed calm, and her
detestation grew. She hated everything about her: the
yellow curls, the watery blue eyes, the voice, the hands.
She hated her own comb when the other had used it, the
fork she ate with, the glass she drank from. At night she
would lie awake, choking with hatred, as she listened to
the other's breathing.

She tried to do something about her feeling. She
thought she was being low and mean and sometimes
still more detestable than Helga. She thought she was
a petty-minded little vixen, just because she resented
someone else using her hairbrush, her cigarettes, her
potatoes, her soap. Then again, she would wax indignant
that the blond Helga was sponging off her, even though
Helga had more money and nicer clothes. Her indig-
nation was followed by the fear that she had an envious
nature. She felt ashamed of herself, she thought she was

being unfair to her cousin, and she did violence to her feelings by being nice to her. Her hatred grew. Lenchen became increasingly bewildered. She missed the nice man and learned that Helga was to blame. "You should be pleased," she said, "didn't you tell me yourself you didn't really hit it off. Anyway, you're not alone, aren't I here with you?" Lenchen dreamed of coming home from work and being informed by a neighbor that Helga had unexpectedly died. Gradually, she ceased to care whether Helga offered her objective reasons to dislike her or not. She could no longer stand the sight of her, she didn't want to breathe the same air as her, she hated her blindly and unconditionally. One day she crushed eight sleeping pills into her mulled wine. Helga didn't die, but she did spend the next three days in hospital, and Lenchen had to confront an ugly charge. She defended herself clumsily and made a bad impression in court, while the blonde was noble, sweet, and sympathetic. To this day, Lenchen doesn't know why she did the thing with the tablets. Maybe she had hoped the bane of her life would sicken and disappear, maybe she even hoped she would die, maybe—oh Lord, what did she know. Her own life, anyway, was one huge mess. She had gone to jail and lost her job, and now she was locked out of her own flat. Her enemy was there now with a fun-loving friend from work.

At the time Lenchen came to see me, she was down to her last five marks. She had seen the word "advice" on a sign. At first, she had just wanted to ask if I could find another job for her, then, haltingly and confusedly, she had told me the story of her lapse. I was able to find a place for her for a week with Fräulein Kuckuck, our graphologist. The first three days are gone, and now Lenchen is afraid she'll be as much of a nuisance for Fräulein Kuckuck as Helga was for her. Maybe I'm prejudiced, but it seems to me the butter-blonde was all sweet deceit and unappealing. She disgusted me.

Johanna is a good girl. When I told her about Lenchen, she even briefly forgot about Anton. "What a silly thing," she said, "if she hadn't been such a scaredy-cat with that blond bitch, and so timid and anxious, but had made a proper stink and thrown her out on her ear—well, then she wouldn't have accumulated so much hatred in her, and she'd never have tried to kill her. Do you understand now, Ferdinand, how humane and beneficial a well-timed slap can be?" I must say, I didn't quite, because one can not do the one without doing the other, but for all I knew, Johanna might have a point.

Johanna proposed an approach to Magnesius. He was to employ Lenchen as a typist, find her a room, and then later, with a lawyer, get the blonde out of her apartment.

Magnesius is a hard-boiled character, but Johanna was still able to get the better of him on occasion. Only this time, I didn't really fancy her chances. Faced with

a real murderess Magnesius would get collywobbles.
"But he's half a murderer himself," said Johanna, "if
not more. How often do you think he wished a business
rival might catch the bubonic plague, and how many
times he hoped to see someone dead whom he hadn't
been able to swindle?" I didn't doubt it. But between
the wish and its fulfillment lies a long and decisive
way. "The only thing the world cares about is if the
deed succeeds or not," said Johanna. Her empathy with
Lenchen the moral train wreck started to frighten me.
The least objection on my part caused her to argue like
a mass murderer on the loose.

"Basically, you're a mass murderer yourself," Johanna
claimed, pouring the last of the brandy into our glasses.
"Imagine you had a button, Ferdinand. Don't look so
stupid, I mean, a simple little button, like a bell push that
you carried around in your pocket. Whenever you want
someone to die, you just reach into your pocket and press
the button, and whoever it is drops dead—no pain, no suffering, just one last breath, and out out brief whatsit."

I told Johanna I would never press such a button.
"Of course you would, Ferdinand, and how. Maybe you'd
feel some compunction the first few times, but you'd
get over it. Remember that hypocritical minister who
was on the radio for hours the other day—"I could kill
him," you said. I bet you'd have pressed the button even
while he was speaking. You'd have done it with pleasure.

And right now, because you've a soft spot for Lenchen, you've conceived a hatred for that disgusting blond moth-head. Imagine, just pushing a button, and your friend's worries are over. You'd press the button twenty times just reading the newspaper. You'd wipe out oily editors, twisted judges, deceitful, slanderous women, animal tormentors, politicians of every stripe, nuclear physicists, weapon salesmen, slave drivers, and war-mongers." I refused to accept the imputation of so much active philanthropy. Johanna wouldn't yield. "You would wipe them out with your button. The only reason you're not doing it now is because it's against the law, because you'd be punished, because it's difficult, and because actually doing it would be unpleasant. I completely believe that you wouldn't want to be responsible for the death of someone who was a mortal enemy or bop them on the head with an ax. Thank God, even today you're not the only person to draw the line at that. But with my button you'd have a way of killing people casually and impersonally—it wouldn't even be murder, you'd just be removing them from the planet."

Johanna went on and on elaborating her conjecture with the button. In her imagination, I'd already depop-ulated half the planet, including the Hunsrück farmer who gave me five pounds of maggoty flour in exchange for my last pair of shoes. "Now, Ferdinand, just picture a couple of starving fools, you can smell the lost war on them three blocks away, they get stomach cramps at the sight of a delicatessen window, and then one of those slimy politicians drives past in his socking great Maybach, just composing his latest pimping address to the electorate—are you telling me you wouldn't push the button? You'd be ashamed not to." I admit to not being entirely positive what I'd do under those circumstances, but Johanna still won't give up. "Name me one person, Ferdinand, who would never push the button if he had one."

"I expect there'd be some, Johanna."

Johanna laughs. "Oh, really? Well, tell me the name—just one person known to us both. Are you claiming your fiancée Luise and your old in-laws wouldn't have pushed it ten times in a week? Or Magnesius. Your friend, that sweet-natured Heinrich? At the very least he'd have put his enemy to sleep, that scandal-sheet editor who's forever having a go at him. He'd have begun with him. Your cheerful landlady Frau Stabhorn would have cut a swath through the ranks of police and customs inspectors. Do you suppose there'd be a pretty woman left under forty if Meta Kolbe had the button? Give it to Liebezahl and check after an hour how many people are left in the tax office. Maybe a charlady, at best."

I was getting bored with the button schtick. "I don't want your button, Johanna—anyway, it doesn't exist, and there's no point in talking about such a thing."

"It's not pointless, Ferdinand, I want you to see that it's just a matter of chance that you're not a much more prolific murderer than Lenchen. You shouldn't give yourself airs in relation to her. Admit it, that's what you're doing. You want to help her the way you help a fallen woman. That's no good to her. She feels it, maybe subconsciously, but she feels it. All right, she's having difficulty in her life. If that's a flaw, it's one you have too. You have no reason to be condescending just because you're managing to eat by playing the village idiot adviser for Liebezahl." Johanna beamed at me. Once she'd stopped banging at me with her wooden hammer, the world seemed light and pleasant again. "I've got an end of gin, Ferdinand, and I propose we drink that now, then we'll head off—you to Anton, and me first to Magnesius, then to Lenchen. Maybe I'll drop in on the blond bint and tear out some of her hair, if I can fit her in."

Johanna's movements were cheerful and brisk. She wore a fluffy purple dress and looked like a rampaging campanula. I didn't have the strength to get in her way. She was looking forward to tonight, she said, she had never supposed she would be looking forward to silly Anton. She didn't have the least doubt that I would be able to produce Anton right away. It never failed to impress me when someone had such confidence in me.

"I swear I'll get him for you!" I exclaimed, fueled by the cooking brandy. "Do you love him so much, or why

do you want him back so badly, Johanna?" I asked a little
later, because in my mind's eye I could see Anton with
his shovel hands, his sticking-out ears, and his rather
witless expression.

"I'm not afraid anymore when he's around," came
Johanna's reply, "not of life, nor of death."

It was stupid of me to forget that everyone, even
Johanna, is born with some kind of fear. No one can
take away such a fear, no more than they could take away
your heart without killing you. But if Anton is capable of
taking away Johanna's fear, that makes him an important figure in her life. So if it's up to me, she can have
him. "You know, the sort of fear you don't know where it
comes from, that's real fear, and I don't have that when
Anton's around," she said, powdering her face. "I'm
still afraid of bombs and diseases and the man from the
electricity company who'll cut me off because I haven't
paid the bill—but that's a different fear, that's a fear I can
touch with my hands."

"Let's go, Johanna," I said, "before we get even
drunker, let's not lose ourselves in metaphysics." I felt a
bit rotten. It's so easy being a spoilsport, shutting off the
living font of a woman's ideas with a well-timed fancy
word and an off-the-peg philosophical term.

"Call it metaphysics if you like, Ferdinand, if you
can't find any words of your own, you puny creature,"
said Johanna. Bless her—at the very last moment, she

always stops you feeling too guilty in front of her. "Will you get my Anton?"

"Yes, Johanna, I'll get him for you."

The evening was ripe and round as I traipsed through the park on the way to Anton. The air already had a distinctly autumnal smell. I was sad the lindens weren't flowering anymore, I love their smell, and I didn't get enough of it while it was going. And this summer I didn't hear a nightingale either.

I loved the shimmering planes of lawn, the sound of my own footfall, and the colorless sky getting to be night. I thought about Johanna's death button and the fact that I might be prepared to press it so as not to meet Anton's deadly potato aunt.

I thought about Lenchen. She came to see me again today, the pale flower.

"I didn't really know what I could ask you and how, Herr Timpe," she said, "I thought your business might be shady, or for all I know obvious, do you understand? See, I've just come out of prison. It's a wonderful thing to be free; I feel so happy. Of course, I'm unhappy as well. I went to the labor exchange. It felt funny, having to stand in line like a beggar in a soup kitchen—just for permission to work. They told me there that I would have to be patient. I found all that a bit humiliating. Don't you agree? Please tell me if I'm boring you, Herr Timpe? I'm afraid I can't even pay you anything. I thought you might

be able to tell me how you get to be a prostitute. You
know, I'm so happy to be free again, I'm so happy not to
be in prison, and I want to enjoy the feeling. I don't want
to kill myself. As long as possible, I don't. Do you understand? If someone had asked me a couple of years ago if
I'd rather be in prison or dead, I'd have said I'd rather be
dead. No question. But now I've survived prison. I expect
I'd survive being a prostitute too. But I'd have to try it
out first, I can always kill myself later."

Outside, there was a woman waiting, something
about a daybed. Her mother-in-law had caused it to sag
and ruined it in other ways too. Now the mother-in-law
was refusing to pay her share of the reconditioning ex-
penses. The woman wanted to discuss the case with me,
and she was starting to get impatient.

I advised Lenchen not to go into prostitution, it
really wasn't a nice life. "Good God," said Lenchen, "I'm
not kidding myself, I was just keeping it in reserve for
when things got really rough. I think I'm getting there,
mind. Please don't misunderstand me. I just wanted to
tell you that getting started in prostitution is surprisingly hard. When I think of the old newspaper articles
I used to read, it seemed almost more difficult not to.
Every servant girl was in grave danger. Don't you remember articles like 'White Slaves Exported'? But if
you want to set up in the trade here, domestically, whom
do you ask? Do you suppose the welfare office has any

information? Or the police? All the magazines have their mailbags that claim to answer all sorts of questions, but I don't think they would answer mine. And you either can't or won't give me an answer yourself. Of course, I've heard of these places called brothels, but I don't know where a single one of them is. Do you suppose a girl can just go there and introduce herself? I never thought I was particularly clever, but I didn't think I was that ignorant either."

I think for the moment Lenchen has given up her idea of becoming a call girl. I'm sure she wouldn't be good at it. Then again, most people follow professions they're no good at. I try to discuss Lenchen's plans objectively with her. With someone who's really in the soup, it's no good going to them with your ethical concerns and prejudices. I'm just glad she hasn't managed so far to gain admittance to those circles. Extraordinary, really, the way each profession is armored in its own exclusiveness, and you don't get to join it without some kind of entrée. Not long ago an agreeable middle-aged man came to see me, a man you could smell came from a good background, modest and with pleasant manners. So far as I can remember, he had been a house tutor in Breslau, and with his family managed to find temporary asylum with landed relatives outside Cologne. After a protracted struggle with himself, he had decided to become a taxi driver. Like many others, he had the rather touching notion that such an obvious social climbdown would be interpreted as a noble sacrifice, and accordingly compensated and admired. Whereas in fact, if the poor fellow has no friends among the taxi-driving fraternity, he won't even get any useful advice. I pulled a few strings and introduced him to the Rose Guzzler. The Rose Guzzler is an old taxi driver, somewhere between fifty and seventy. I don't know his real name. It wouldn't surprise me if he didn't either. Like most of the veterans in his profession, his nickname grew over his name. And where does that come from? Maybe once in the days of his youth he had an accident with a rosebush or he drove into a pond with sea roses, or some uncouth colleagues caught him in the act of pressing a rose to his lips that some winsome girl had given him. The roughest fellows are often exposed to such lyrical shocks. And *Carmen* will never go out of fashion.

I've known the Rose Guzzler for years. On the back of his left hand he has the tattoo of a fly, delicate and pert. Maybe in his previous life he knew Pompadour, or he even *was* Pompadour. If one believes in the transmigration of souls, then why impose limits; everything is possible. People who believe in miracles shouldn't try and rein in their imaginations. In for a penny, in for a pound, I say. Just at the moment that poor Brylcreemed Gröning is being hailed as a miracle worker.* The press is coining it, and so are the press barons. Instead of a beating, they are raking it in. I've no idea what old Brylcreem-head is making. I'm only astonished by the modesty of the thousands of believers streaming to see a creature who is no more miraculous than they are. A proper miracle doctor, in my book, is someone who will cut my head off and reattach it, he will turn a tree trunk into a flesh and blood leg, he will cure my depression by changing my pocket lint into thousand-mark notes. "One shouldn't demand the impossible," people said to me when they asked me if they should seek out this Gröning.

"Of course you should demand the impossible," I countered, "you don't come to some sort of compromise with a miracle, you ask for everything—absolutely everything." Why shouldn't I believe in miracles? Everything's possible. Only I can't respect the kind of thing I've already encountered in the course of my life. The fact that a thing may resist explanation isn't enough for me. At other times, everything seems like a miracle—my own existence, the earth, the stars, people, trees. Just now, actually being dead seems the greatest miracle to me. I don't want to become an angel or a devil or a ghost—or for that matter an owl, a swallow, a

---

* German mystic Bruno Gröning (1906–59) became a media sensation in 1949 following reports that he had miraculously healed a young boy in the town of Herford. He preached that human beings could recharge their natural energy by tapping into a higher power he called the "healing stream" (*Heilstrom* in German).

seal, or a lilac bush. One is inclined to envy all forms of existence other than one's own. I expect a lilac bush is consumed with anxiety. It maybe doesn't like earthworms, and they're gathering round its roots. It flowers, because that's in its contract, and then the little moths sit on its blossoms without so much as a by-your-leave. I want to be absolutely nothing at all, that too is something I want to experience and enjoy. I want the unassimilable. I want to have the experience of not being able to experience anything—I want to enjoy the fact that there's no more enjoyment for me. I want eternal existence in complete dissolution. I want something that will boil off all the possibilities of my imagination. I want the miracle that exists beyond dream and thought. The truly miraculous is the unthinkable. If something is thinkable, then it's at best a fairy story. All fairy stories were or will one day be true. They are the product of experience and intuition. They are assertions that became or will become proofs.

As I walked along, I wished I could walk for days, and then fall down and sleep for the rest of infinity.

I felt wrapped up in my life as in a light, rustling integument. Sometimes it seems heavy, dirty, and wrinkled, just at the moment it seemed clean and silky smooth. My time alone showed me an intoxicating parade of fleeting yearnings, and a power of imagination that allowed me to treat them as genuine and available.

The thoughts in my brain were whirling like dust motes in the wind—they were so flighty I wasn't even tempted to try and hold on to them. Nor did I want to exert myself or go to any trouble, but just to be left alone, like a child who wanted to play.

Unfortunately, I didn't have long for my communion with myself. Already, I was insufficiently isolated to ignore the calls from outside. It was getting late, and Johanna wanted her Anton back. I like to take the requirements of my friends seriously, even if they strike me as absurd.

On my way, I dropped in on Heinrich. I thought I needed to put on the intellectual corset that the real world makes you wear.

At Heinrich's, the world was all too real. His magazine, *Red Dawn*, has appeared, and Heinrich is already working on the third issue. He was busy with a string of domestic murders. Pride of place went to a woman who popped her husband's head in a shopping bag and later bought Brussels sprouts. That sort of thing seems to be in these days. Heinrich assures me that readers like nothing better than murders and sex crimes. Flashers in public parks are always useful. With headlines like "Disgusting Menace," the magazine wears its morality on its sleeve. Improper pictures, preferably from abroad, come in handy, so long as the magazine prints bold subtitles saying "We reject horrid images like these!"

Red Dawn has become exactly the publication Heinrich never wanted it to become. Once, he was revolted by the flood of half-disguised scandal sheets without originality or freshness. Now he finds his *Red Dawn* upstanding and courageous.

What is it that drives newspapers to depict the world as a shuddersome freak show? The authenticated birth of a two-headed baby is enough to set editors yelping with joy. Mad, distorted reports are carried, ideally from remote places, so as to elude the inquiries of fanatical pedants.

I try to supply Heinrich with a few leads: Three-year-old toddler bites lion to death in jungle clearing. Ninety-year-old Tibetan woman leaps off thirty-foot rock every day in bid to remain supple. Bedouin keeps tame duck as secretary, types his worldwide correspondence for him. Three sardines hatched alive from purple hen's egg in Texas. Man seeks divorce after wife abandons him in bowl of unsalted spinach. Hundred-and-three-year-old Bavarian woman leaves suicide note, complaining that world too annoyingly moral to be endured. Bull swallows Caruso record in Mexico and starts singing; torero moved to tears. Albanian man celebrates one-hundred-and-eightieth birthday swimming underwater for hours, laughing.

Heinrich says he will consider the one about the bull. Next, I proposed a few "handy hints for household and personal grooming." Angel-hair noodles woven into the hair nourish the scalp and give their wearer a silky sheen. The juice of half a melon dripped down the neck of a returning husband is an ideal prewash. Moths will never go near china that has been dropped from the balcony in mild weather. Floor mats last longer when pushed under wardrobes.

Not all my suggestions met with Heinrich's approval. Editors always think they're not doing their job if they drop their pose of rejection and criticism. I can understand my brother the night porter when he turned his back on literature.

Heinrich was still considering the quiz for readers. I offered him a few obvious questions:

To our fair-minded male and female and other readers: towards the end of your life in a closed institution, do you still expect to have sex appeal? Then answer the following questions and tot up your scores at the end. One. Do you feel insecure when you sit on a beer mat? Two. Would you eat a chrysanthemum if you were offered goulash? Three. Have you ever felt moved to bite a stork in the leg? Four. Has it come to your notice that the town of Bebra has never appeared in a song? Five. If you were born in Bebra, do you think you would be proud of the fact? Could you imagine in the course

of a vacation under orange blossoms and mimosas
by the sunny Mediterranean, sighing, O my Bebra!?

"We can't have that," said Heinrich. "That last one would make the reader suspicious, it's too complicated, he would think it was an attack and he would feel offended."

I agreed to scrub question five. "It has to be ten questions," said Heinrich, and he sent me a look that was both anxious and a little exhausted.

Briefly I pondered how much the love of homeland of a German city dweller could persist if he were set down in a beet field in rainy November. Nothing against "love of soil," but there have to be limits, even if it is entirely imaginary. Imaginary love is admittedly more obdurate than real love because it springs from some deviated sense of self that takes itself for idealism. Most people fall for this hook, line, and sinker as soon as they lose their innocence concerning this mistake and recognize that it is a mistake. Harmless believers usually become fanatics if they are no longer able to believe what they once thought was a good idea. Whoever seeks to preserve a conviction against the available evidence will ultimately resort to evil. He must convince others of at least a fraction of his own belief. The less he is able to do so, the more furious he will become.

At the end of his day, Heinrich likes to immerse himself in half-baked philosophy. But today he hadn't

knocked off yet and was still mixing his literary cocktail for his *Red Dawn* readership. I had no great desire
to offer Heinrich my services as mixologist, but I was
even less inclined to see Anton. I was looking for an
ethical excuse for my delay. Often, I will do something
disagreeable purely so as not to have to do something
still more disagreeable. Besides, I was just now feeling
extremely idle. The thought of the to me little-known
Anton was more of a strain than Heinrich. In spite of it
all, I felt obliged to move for a speedy departure.

"Write one more piece under the rubric 'Unusual
Experiences of a Female Reader,'" I said to Heinrich.
"Our reader Karla Pickbock sent us the following: 'At
the suggestion of a friend I went to see a football match
a year ago. The crowd was largely male, and I had the
strange feeling they were there for me. After I let the last
tram leave without me, a gentleman asked me if I knew
how to roller skate. The question sealed my fate. Today I
am happily married and the mother of three strapping
lads, who leave me no time for roller skating. I wish my
sisters a similar fate.'"

"Such true-life experiences are both relevant and
ethical," observed Heinrich. "With a few little nips and
tucks I can use them." He transcribed, with a few nips
and tucks. His features showed the tragically iced-
over resolve of those self-sacrificial beings who have

to rescue thousands upon thousands of others' bodies, souls included.

Once I had convinced Heinrich of the literary stimulus of a visit to Anton and his aunt, he agreed to accompany me there.

The aunt was charming. I have no idea what Johanna finds so scary about her. While Anton kept us waiting for ten minutes, she served us apple cake and *Korn*. She's a doughty old girl of seventy or so, with a thoroughly modern attitude. She plays the football pools and goes to freestyle wrestling. Where the current crop of magazine publications is concerned, she deplored the plethora of beautiful naked young girls and women. Not that she had any ethical doubts. Her point was merely that most of the readership was female, and the woman customer was heavily emphasized. Didn't she also have a right to be considered in the advertising? No normal woman was continually interested in the chests and legs of other women. It hurt her self-respect to have to spend money on them. In a word, the aunt was requesting the male pinup. She was herself long past the years of fleshly desire, but she would still like to see women getting their deserts. Heinrich left, deeply impressed by the doughty fighter, when Anton finally appeared and I pushed him out onto the street.

The conversation with Anton took place in the corner pub. Johanna had given me a false account of the case of Gustav. Anton had seen her perched on his lap. I suggested that she was working on his rheumatism. Unfortunately, Anton showed himself impervious to medical arguments. Johanna will say it didn't mean anything. She's not even lying when she claims such a thing. She is lavish in her orientation. Hers is a generous nature; what members of women's groups would see as a volcanic outbreak of sinful passion to her is a minor bagatelle.

It was child's play, well below the dignity of an ambitious psychologist, to bring Anton round to Johanna's way of seeing things. He was dying to be persuaded and couldn't wait to run around to Johanna's.

Johanna was playing host to Lenchen, the pallid flower. She seemed shy and timid, like an orphan being inspected by a committee and required to recite a poem. She seemed capable neither of murder nor of the reckless intention to pursue the calling of a hunter of men.

From Magnesius, Johanna had collected a tin of pineapple, a bottle of bubbly, four packs of Chesterfields, and the promise to employ Lenchen in his business sometime soon. That was about all I was able to glean from her. Soon she was busy with Anton.

The relatives
are coming

.
.
.

❦

.
.
.

Some of my siblings have already
arrived. I can love someone to the
point of insanity and miss them
like fury, but I hate meeting them
at the station. All my siblings hate
to be met at the station. In spite of
that, I still feel obliged to go and
meet each new arrival. And each

new arrival feels obliged to tell me when they're coming, so that I can be there to meet them.

The first to arrive was the beautiful Aloisia. She is still beautiful. If anything, she's even more radiant than she was before. And I had expected to meet a physical and emotional wreck. I had dreaded meeting Aloisia. A year ago, Aloisia's husband, Hugo Moppe, died. Hugo Moppe's death shattered us, but only because of Aloisia. Even Leberecht in far-off Brazil was convinced that Aloisia would rapidly fade away and follow Hugo into the grave in the space of a year.

One isn't supposed to speak ill of the dead, though I don't really know why. If someone dies, it doesn't make him any better. And it's not really the dead man one speaks ill of, so much as his living placeholder. I am unable to say whether Hugo Moppe is pleasanter or more likable now as a corpse or ghost than he was before. All I remember is the living man, the way he was when I met him in Bonn, and he was a nightmare. By comparison to him, Johanna's Anton is a marvel of handsome spirituality, a fiery intellect, a dazzling raconteur, an inexhaustible font of wisdom and deep kindness.

It was when we were living with Uncle Kuno in Bonn that Hugo Moppe first put in an appearance. I no longer know who unearthed him. I was certainly innocent.

At the time Moppe was an assistant in a pharmacy in Bonn. I know that pharmacists are honorable, pleasant, helpful, and generally saintly people. I know that. But ever since I met Moppe, I've first had to fight back inner shudders whenever I run into one.

If I'd merely run into Moppe somewhere, I couldn't have had any objection to him. His case only became acute through his association with Aloisia. Originally, he was as pallid, colorless, and uninteresting as a washed-out pair of pajama bottoms. But what is a sensible man going to hold against a pair of pajama bottoms, especially if they're not his? He will only start to assume a posture of aggression once they're hung over his lamp as a form of decor, and he is required to admire them, instead of merely getting rid of them.

Aloisia, whose function in life was to get herself admired for her mild, tranquil beauty by all comers, fell in love with Hugo Moppe. In all her born days she had never taken the initiative: with Moppe she did. I still remember how impressed I was when she poured his tea and buttered his bread. I believe it was the first time her hands had ever held a teapot. Next, I was struck when she went into a pharmacy to buy an unguent. Moppe suffered from eczema, in a sort of pallid characterless version. In her whole life, Aloisia had never bought anything herself. Never had she invited anyone to come or go or stay. She asked Moppe to supper every night. He came, and he ate. He spoke little and showed no signs of being in love with Aloisia. I don't believe he even found her beautiful. Perhaps I'm being unfair, but I don't believe he was capable of finding anything beautiful anywhere. Dusty and a little mulish, he sat with us and was far and away the most boring table companion we had ever had. He was so deeply charmless that Laura was once moved to one of her rare outbursts of passion. She said, "That Moppe is no good to man or beast."

We puzzled our heads endlessly as to what Aloisia saw in him. Our whole family was stumped, and it never occurred to Aloisia to help us. The more she sensed the general rejection, the more stubbornly she displayed attention and affection to her idol. The idol let it wash over him. The only time I saw Moppe indicate anything like passion was when he declared Wellingtons practical in rainy weather, and that he had a weakness for crepes.

Of course, we tried everything to drive a wedge between Aloisia and Moppe. But it had the opposite effect. And she had such a splendid selection of admirers. Perhaps she didn't want to be admired. Perhaps she was even looking for someone who didn't see her beauty. If only she hadn't married him. But one day she stepped forward and said she was engaged to be married to him. Probably it was she who proposed, and he was good enough to accept. The worst of it was that Moppe came from a place called Anklam and was going to take over his father's pharmacy—the pokiest and most pitiful pharmacy in all Anklam, as Luitpold once wrote after a visit there. Places

like Anklam exist in the world, and they too will have
their charms. Nothing against Anklam. But to spend one's
life in Anklam with Hugo Moppe and a wretched pharmacy is something one wouldn't wish upon a person who
has done one no wrong.

Aloisia wanted it that way. She moved in with Moppe
in Anklam. At least if the bloody pharmacy had been in
Munich or Berlin. Then there might have been a chance
that one day a fairy-tale prince might have appeared to
rescue Aloisia. To begin with, we continued to think in
those terms, and believed that one day Aloisia would
awaken from her sorry spell. Later on, we gave up that
belief. She kept on declaring that she was content, and
we had to believe her. Anyone visiting her would see her
by turns in the shop and at home, always hard at work.
She scrubbed the steps and darned Moppe's underwear.
She wore burlap aprons and patched rather unglamorous
dresses. She pampered Moppe. She suffered when he
had a cold and was miserable when he cut his finger. Her
whole life revolved around him. For us it looked like a
study in grey. One could almost have wished that Moppe
were a drinker and beat Aloisia. That would have been
something. But he didn't drink, and he didn't hit her.
Dull, apathetic, and indifferent, he accepted her and did
his tedious work. We decided we would view Aloisia as
one of the great lovers in history, a miracle and a rid-
dle. She didn't even get pregnant to lighten her life. She

seemed not to miss being a mother, being apparently altogether fulfilled by Moppe.

And then, about a year ago, Hugo Moppe died. He had survived the war. Flat feet kept him from being drafted. He died of fish poisoning. Ever the miser, he had tucked into some leftover fish salad that was past its best, and which he knew Aloisia meant to throw away.

I didn't feel sorry for Moppe, I felt sorry for Aloisia's death when I heard the news of Hugo's passing. It was clear to me that my sister would either kill herself or die of natural causes in short order. I didn't have the money to visit her. Uncle Kuno was with her, and Luitpold. Both of them tried to whisk her away, but she insisted on staying in Anklam. She couldn't tear herself away from Moppe's graveside, we thought. She was very calm, we could hear that. "Eerily calm," they say in such situations.

We're not a family of letter writers, and Aloisia was always the laziest of us anyway. She wired me the time of her expected arrival. I was surprised she could stand to leave Anklam at all, site of the pharmacy and Moppe's mortal remains. Perhaps, before she withered away entirely, she wanted to see the family one last time.

I know that none of my siblings care to stay with Elfriede. But then I thought that Aloisia, the grief-stricken widow, would fare well there. Elfriede was delighted to have her noble Good Samaritanism validated by the mourning Aloisia. The rest of us had passed the hat around so that she was only accountable for the emotional upkeep.

On the platform I found myself being hugged by a beautiful lady. She seemed fresh, healthy, radiant, and confident. Was Aloisia just pretending? But even the most gifted disguise has its limits. I felt like someone prepared inside and out for a funeral who unpredictably walks into a carnival. I almost had the feeling that Aloisia was making fun of me. I needed fully an hour before I had adjusted to this unexpected Aloisia and was able to enjoy her.

From the get-go, there was a dully swelling enmity between Elfriede and Aloisia. It made Elfriede almost ill when her highly polished Christian qualities suddenly had no employment. She had even put out an old picture of Moppe on Aloisia's nightstand and garnished it with flowers and black ribbons. "Oh, my Lord, Moppe," said Aloisia blithely, "what did you want to put him up for?" For the first time I could feel Elfriede's alienation.

Aloisia was cheerfulness itself. She bought new dresses, she put on makeup, she tried out extravagant hairdos, and she flirted. Even with Elfriede's minister husband.

On her fourth morning, she guzzled a bottle of champagne in Elfriede's kitchen before moving to a hotel. That's where she still is, cheerful and content, visiting me at Liebezahl's and spending a lot of time with Johanna. She's not manically cheerful, as had been my initial fear, just happy, sensible, and with her feet on the ground.

Aloisia has money because she was able to realize a good profit from the sale of the pharmacy in Anklam. Even Magnesius, with whom she discussed further plans, thinks she is businesslike and takes her seriously. Which is saying something. She wouldn't dream of ever setting foot in Anklam again as long as she lives, she told me.

Curiosity can make a fellow ill-mannered. "Do you think of Moppe still?" I asked Aloisia when she was sitting in my room at Liebezahl's one evening.

"Why would I?" replied Aloisia. "Oh, Ferdinand, I know what you mean, I know what you want to hear. Elfriede thinks it's bad of me not to mourn him—you don't think it's bad, but you don't really understand it either. It's just I'm not mourning him. I don't understand why you have to have detailed explanations for everything. Elfriede would be happy to learn that I'd lived like a martyr at Hugo's side, and that he'd treated me terribly. That would just about buy me the right to perk up a bit after his death. But he didn't maltreat me, and I didn't suffer through him. Accordingly, I ought to be suffering now that he's dead. But I'm not suffering. I feel great. Moppe doesn't exist for me anymore. I don't think of him in the daytime unless someone makes me, and at night

I haven't once had a dream with him. Elfriede wouldn't
approve, but she could just about understand it if I were
numbing my terrible pain with all this wild, desperate
pleasure-seeking, and one day collapsed in a madhouse.
But believe me, Ferdinand, I don't have anything to
numb. I know none of you could stand Moppe. I know he
was a boring zero. I suppose I saw something different in
him than the rest of you. There's nothing unusual about
that—everyone means something different to everyone.
And even if you threaten to beat my brains out, I can't
tell you if I loved him or not. Maybe I did, maybe I didn't,
I don't know. At any rate, he occupied me, and above all
he attracted me. Why and how is something I've never
bothered my head about. It seemed pointless to me to try
and solve a puzzle that no one has ever been able to solve.
Anyway, the attraction he had for me when he was alive,
now that he's dead, he doesn't have it anymore. He didn't
leave the least aftertaste—I can barely remember what
he looked like, and it doesn't interest me. I told Elfriede
all that, and she thought I was reprehensible. God knows
why she has to get involved in all these things that don't
concern her. The only thing that might be reprehensible is that I refuse to put on an act for the sake of some
stupid convention. Oh, and by the way, I've got a date
with Magnesius tonight. I know you all take him for a
cunning profiteer and all-round bad hat—but I see him
differently. I think he's nice and I quite like him."

The next morning, Elfriede came to see me. She was deathly pale and deadly serious. "My dear brother," she began, "I hope to goodness you can soon free yourself from this awful, wicked circle, and find some more dignified profession. If you turn your mind to it, I'm sure you can. Even in our family, there are many good and positive energies, some of which have unfortunately been misdirected. But truly, I think only Aloisia and Johanna are past saving."

I got a little impatient. Waiting for me outside my office I had, among others, a man with broken fingernails, a winegrower who wanted to get married for the fourth time, a girl who had been beaten by her mother with a curtain rod, five deserted wives, and a sixth who wished to be deserted because her husband snored. I had my work cut out for me. At lunchtime I was supposed to be meeting Lenchen, and in the evening I was picking up my brother Toni at the station. Before that, I urgently had to see my fiancée Luise.

Luise enthusiastically made common cause with Aloisia. I am a little surprised she feels drawn to the Aloisia of today, it doesn't quite make sense to me. But then what makes sense? Aloisia thinks Luise is charming. That doesn't mean much. At the moment, Aloisia likes anyone who likes her.

I sniffed at the bunch of roses that our pretty graphologist, Fräulein Kuckuck, put out for me. Of late she has an advice-needing admirer who is bombarding her with trainloads of roses. She can no longer cope with them herself and has taken to distributing them in the nearby offices.

"Keep it short, Elfriede," I say in the kindly but inflexible tones of a busy expert. "Is it your husband?"

"What makes you say such a thing?" replies Elfriede, "nothing's the matter with him. Of course, it was mean of Aloisia to call him sweetie, and of Felix to let it pass—but you know how magnanimous I am, Ferdinand." This was actually news to me, but I didn't say anything.

My time-wasting relation carried on like this for a while, till I made her aware that from now on every minute of her being here would set her back. Thus far her presence had set me back, from now it was going to be her money.

Elfriede told me she had received a letter from Uncle Kuno to the effect that it might be a few more days till he and Laura and possibly others would be here. By chance, Laura had seen a Negro toddler in an orphanage, and wanted to keep him. Then, while Uncle Kuno was busy with the paperwork, Laura had seen a second Negro child that also found favor with her.

Why should Laura not take a liking to Negro children? Negro children are delightful. I can't imagine any normal woman who wouldn't be crazy about the little chocolate bonbons that go skipping around on two legs. "I'd like to take her too," Laura will have said calmly. "Kuno, will you see to it." The Negro children will be well looked after by Laura and will be happy with her.

"Not that I have any objection," said Elfriede, who evidently did have objections. Laura wouldn't raise the children properly, Laura had no idea about the raising of children. Laura had so many children of her own she sometimes couldn't remember their names.

I still didn't know what was so riling Elfriede. I think something like this: one sews dresses and buys Bibles for Negro children, one doesn't adopt them. Elfriede might have been troubled by the circus-like aspect of Laura's road shows. I will admit we used to give the impression of a group of tumblers when we traveled with Laura as children.

Maybe Elfriede doesn't think Laura ought to have the Negro children, without knowing it herself. Perhaps she is tormented by the thought of people who always know what they want and act accordingly. Not many people know what gives them joy in life, and I'm sure Elfriede will never be among them.

"Children aren't toys," said Elfriede. Good God, there are people to whom the whole world is a toy, and who love it and take it as seriously and carefully as they take their toys.

"Elfriede," I said, "to me it's a terrible thought that a couple will embark on the production of a future school inspector or structural engineer only after mature reflection and with grim seriousness. Fifty-year-old structural engineers are only rarely pleasant toys, though they might like to have the feeling they once were." Elfriede remarked coldly that she regretted that she couldn't join me in my outlandish notions. Maybe she really did regret it. I gave her three red roses and saw her to the door.

In the astrological scents department, I could hear Elfriede in discussions with Liebezahl. "This is an unusually discreet perfume," said Liebezahl, "but its effect on the opposite sex can be extremely strong, and may cause you to be molested, Madam—I see it as my duty to make you aware of the risk."

"Pah, a decent woman can always stand up for herself—I mean, as long as the perfume has a soothing effect on the wearer—" Elfriede began to stammer.

"Of course, of course—naturally . . ." I could hear the bow in Liebezahl's voice. Elfriede had made the purchase.

That evening, my attendance was required at the first meeting of Eulogies for the Living. Liebezahl founded it, of course with a beady eye to the financial interests of his overall enterprise. I don't quite understand how Liebezahl hasn't collapsed under the weight of so

many ideas. Of course, it's a fine thing for a man to have
ideas, but I can't help thinking it would be a fine thing if
Liebezahl would just occasionally spare us.

Eulogies for the Living is in its trial phase just now.
Liebezahl doesn't have terribly high expectations of it,
but he feels obliged to try out each one of his ideas. It has
often happened that ideas that seemed wholly unpracti-
cable and uncommercial later go on to be highly successful. Above all, Liebezahl is able to set them going in
such a way that they don't lose money.

Eulogies for the Living does what it says on the
package. Liebezahl has ascertained that most people
in their lifetimes don't hear much about themselves
that is good. To be celebrated and lauded in the highest
terms, someone first has to be lying in his coffin. Then
he will be regaled with flowers, tears, music, and much
impassioned recognition of his qualities. But what good
is all that to the deceased? Any thinking person must
realize that once dead he will have diminished capacity for enjoyment and understanding. So why not—thus
Liebezahl—move forward the commemoration and
delight the living person?

Of course, it wasn't an altogether straightforward
matter for Liebezahl to find parties for this idea, because
people don't like to be put in mind of death, least of all
their own. So he suggested that society members should
be accounted dead as regarded their lives to date, and a

newer, better life would commence for them. This made play with the ancient wisdom that a person reported to have died has especially long to live.*

Liebezahl spent a week sweating over the promotional literature, trying to make it plain, persuasive, and illuminating. He wanted all departments to recruit for it. Eulogies for the Living already had over a dozen members.

And tonight was the first meeting. Every four weeks the celebratee would be randomly chosen. The first lucky winner was one Bobby Ampel.

Bobby Ampel is a man of thirty-four, but not really. The word "man" doesn't sit well on him. There are males of the species who even at the age of seventy are wizened striplings. Bobby Ampel is a stripling. He has prior convictions for bigamy, misleading a public official, and black marketeering. Other than that, he is an angelic fellow with a heart of gold. The one doesn't exclude the other. Sometimes a degree of viciousness is needed to resist certain temptation. Ampel isn't vicious, he is someone who is constantly fooled by others. Currently, he is leading a rather quiet life in his brother-in-law's candle factory.

Liebezahl's most spacious room was ceremonially decked out in garlands, flowers, drapes, and potted

---

* Like Irmgard Keun herself, when her suicide was reported in 1940 in the UK's *Daily Telegraph*.

palms. In the middle of the room stood a huge garlanded armchair in which Bobby Ampel sat enthroned. In front of him was a lectern with lofty candles at either side. Music was provided by a trio. Mourners sat round the walls, some of them society members, others invited guests. The windows were draped, the only light being provided by the candles on the lectern. A soft scent of incense and roses filled the room. Liebezahl had personally attended to every detail. For publicity reasons, it was important that this first celebration be a particularly impressive occasion.

The band played a tender rendition of "Enjoy your lives . . ." Then the amulet salesman, a resting actor, mounted the podium. His voice trembled with feeling. "And so we end the life to date of our beloved Bobby Ampel. Who could ever hope to truly do justice to the wonderful faculties of this man? Words fail us. His life to date was pure and without stain, sacrificing himself to the good of others. He was a sunbeam in all of our lives. What would we be—what would the world be—without him? Who can think of this kindly heart without emotion? Have we ever thanked him properly? He must and shall remain an example to us for all time. His life was a battle, and one he can be proud of. Bobby Ampel, we will never forget your life's work, your loyalty and unstinting activity, your fiery spirit and proud manhood. You were a font of bliss and a spur to your loved ones, and to your employees the burningly revered ideal of a true leader."

Bobby Ampel had tears in his eyes, and the rest of the room seemed moved as well. The trio played a slow rendition of "By the well at the gate . . . ," and Liebezahl laid down a wreath of cornflowers at Ampel's feet. Other society members, in their Sunday best, followed with bouquets and wreaths. There were further brief addresses and poem recitals, till finally Liebezahl brought the stirring celebration to an end with a few well-chosen words and led the mourners to the pub across the road, with whose landlord he had made a cut-price deal. The wake had a special piquancy because the dear departed, decked with his floral tributes, took full part in it.

Both members and guests seemed to me to have been powerfully impressed, and to crave similar commemoration for themselves. Liebezahl was reasonably satisfied, but thought it needed a few tweaks. Anyway, he had just thought of the next thing.

I went around to Luise, bringing her Fräulein Kuckuck's roses, and for half an hour I didn't know what to talk about with her.

People who don't know how to talk to each other are usually no good at silence either. I am thinking continually of what to say, and don't dare lose myself in my own thoughts.

I tried telling Luise about Bobby Ampel, that
squashed little baby gangster. But Luise doesn't care
for bigamists, and she thinks Liebezahl's field of operations, and hence mine, contemptible. Liebezahl is
used to the reproach that he takes money for his phil-
anthropic actions. "So, am I supposed to starve, then?"
he asked. "Does a doctor not take money for dabbing
the sweat from a fevered brow? Does a poet not take
money when he laments the ancient pain of mankind
in indelible rhythms, and causes our deepest, noblest
feelings to resonate? Maybe not, but then only because
no one was offering him any. Will a violinist or organ-
ist move his listeners to tears for nothing? Will a priest
not accept payment for leading his flock to the throne
of God with kindly zeal? Are all these noble professions
to live off sunshine and fresh air?" Liebezahl probably doesn't take himself as any less deserving than the
noblest helpers and most luminous idols of mankind.
The rascal probably doesn't exist who is unable to come
up with excuses for his profession, which isn't to say
that Liebezahl is a rascal in my book. In the space of
another year he wants to have the most progressive
psychotherapeutic institute in Europe, he is already in
negotiations with doctors who will provide the undertaking with the necessary scientific gravitas. He
predicts a proud future for himself. As a dignified old
man, he may one day look back with a sentimental tear

in his eye for his present happy-go-lucky fairground
business.

Time is weighing heavy on my hands at Luise's.
Again, I find myself wishing I were by myself. But this
wish has become less anguished since my latest thought.
I imagined waking up one morning and being all alone
in the world. All other humans have gone up in a puff
of smoke or dust. In the whole world there is no living
being. No one can bother me, torment me, threaten me.
There is no one. The world has gone quiet, nowhere any
strife, greed, hatred, envy, wickedness. All I hear are
the sounds of the air, and my own breathing. I wander
through the empty streets and buildings. In the kitchen
and pantry of a derelict restaurant I assemble a meal for
myself and drink a bottle of wine. I wander into book-
shops and clothes shops and take what I need, without
having to pay. I stand in the silent station and sit in the
deserted waiting room. Millions of empty beds await
me when it gets dark. If I knew that there was another
human being anywhere in the world, I would race off
to try and find him or her. I would throw myself at the
meanest and lowest creature, sobbing with emotion.
How does the hermit survive? Well, it probably makes a
difference if one has turned one's back on mankind vol-
untarily or was left behind by them. Anyway, the hermit
knows there is no shortage of people, and if he wants to,
he can seek them out whenever he likes. But the further I

traveled over the deserted surface of the earth, the more
deeply I felt the void all around me. Each time I saw anything beautiful, I would feel miserable. I didn't need to
justify the manner of my life to anyone, and I wasn't able
to please or annoy anyone either. I would have a voice for
no reason. I would own everything in the world and own
nothing. Probably I'd be too old to come to any new and
living relation to trees and flowers.

And God? It would be blasphemy to try and make
some stand-in human out of Him. He wouldn't be able
to replace him either. Supposing I believed in Him, I
couldn't even be good for His sake. I think we are made
too accustomed from childhood to seeing God as a kind
of cosmic policeman, striving to regulate the complicated interactions of people.

I have nothing against the fulfillment of wishes. But
sometimes it's good for a wish to remain unfulfilled. As
always, I love being alone. But after thinking through
my dream to the very last consequence, it's become more
of a nightmare, and I'm inclined to see the dullest bore
and most miserable wretch as a life-saving companion.
If, after days or weeks in the deserted world, I were to
run into Luise, I'm sure she would seem anything but
stifling to me. She would help me to attain a new life.
Her foolish mouthing of idiotic pop songs would bring
tears of joy to my eyes. Flowers, mountains, spring,
autumn, books, diamonds, fine wines and good food,

sad thoughts, bad moods, joyful recognition, gentle renunciations, and noisy desires—all these would once again have meaning. Oh, the tides would ebb and flood once more.

I said a very sincere goodbye to Luise.

The party of the broken glasses

. . . . .

Johanna's party began early
in the evening, I don't know
what the time is now. Without
a watch, there's just a spinning
on through alcohol and human
entanglements.

People dance, people sit,
stand, lie around. People come,

and people go. Some seem unfamiliar to me, as though they'd just blown in off the street. For Johanna, it's the presence of strangers that makes it a party.

A radio is playing, two or three gramophones are playing, a young man is belaboring his accordion, a tenor voice rings out loud and off-key. All around there are cushions, and half-full and empty bottles and glasses in amongst broken records.

Everyone seems cheerful, probably they are cheerful too, and I only think of them as sad because I'm sad. I think almost the only thing capable of making me profoundly sad is a party. How do people do it, fall into wild high spirits on command at a preset time? Perhaps their high spirits are forced without them knowing it? They are no longer free, they are prisoners of their intoxication. Forced hilarity makes me sad. Damnit, I don't want to let myself go like this. I'll have another drink, maybe that'll do the trick. I've had quite a bit already. The more I drink, the soberer I feel. Damned alcohol won't let itself be bossed around, it keeps control of you, and you do what it wants. Drinking is a lottery. You never know in advance whether it'll make you merry or sad, loving or angry, gentle or furious, clever or moronic.

How much work Johanna put into this. At least a dozen people were kept busy. I helped too. Sometimes I'm fed up with doing things I have no desire to do.

Johanna's lending library has been turned into a bar, there are colored paper hangings screening the book-shelves, borrowed by the noodle-maker Albert Theodor Peipel from his mother. Her room is all cushions, poufs, and paper chains. Liebezahl's room is stuffed full of sofas. In the yard, walled in by ruins, a long trestle table has been set up. The summer night is warm and pliant.

I am sitting somewhere in the background, perched between two bins. Every five minutes or so, someone in the neighborhood yells "Quiet!" whereupon everyone in the yard sets up an even wilder din.

There is any amount to drink, and all sorts. Of course, Johanna couldn't afford it all. Her business is going very badly, she is in debt, and has no idea what to do about the bailiffs. To be able to devote herself still more fully to Anton in thought and deed, she has neglected her translation work. Women in love run the risk of financial ruin. I am comforted by the thought that so far Johanna has emerged from her calamities fresh and cheerful. She isn't a person who reeks of tragic destiny and imminent end.

Each guest was called upon to bring at least one bottle of wine or spirits. Liebezahl, Heinrich, Peipel, Magnesius, and one or two more will have been charged to bring a five- or tenfold amount. In return, my pallid Lenchen was permitted to come without anything, and Johanna's best friend, Meta Kolbe, with a split of Blue

Nun. "Very strong and good for you, too," she pro-
claimed. I myself have witnessed elderly ladies quietly
and steadily chugging Blue Nun and thinking they were
doing good work and not indulging in the demon drink.
Everything depends on the name of the given product.
You can be a whiskey tippler but never a Blue Nun tippler.

Like many businesspeople, Magnesius is a jovial
and generous party animal, only to emerge as even icier
and stonier later. He damascenes himself. To heighten
the mood, he has jammed a green monocle in one eye,
and pulled a yellow silk stocking over his head. Just now
I saw him kissing the hand of a woman unknown to me
and offering to buy her a brand-new Mercedes.

Several of the gentlemen are going around in paper
hats or capital beer mats. In many men the compulsion
to unconventional head attire becomes uncontrollable
when they have been drinking together. On the whole,
this is a harmless urge and shouldn't be discouraged.
I only wish I knew whence it sprang. For the past hour,
Peipel has sported a tea cozy, which must be burdensome
for him, and calefactory.

The tuneless tenor is bareheaded, only he is singing incessantly, now in the courtyard, now in the room
with the cushions, now in the bar. He was hoping to be
discovered, Johanna tells me. I guess him to be around
fifty, but older men have been discovered. Johanna
asked him because she likes his style and wants to make

him happy. He seems happy enough to me. He can sing
to his heart's content—no one's stopping him and no
one's listening. His name is Damian Hell,* and he's a
postman. Or rather, he used to be a postman, the most
delightful postman in his district. He empathized with
his clients. He was happy when he was able to bring them
post and miserable when they waited in vain for letters,
and he was gifted in the expression of his unhappiness.
He cheered people up, comforted them, and made them
happy with his empathy. The dullest beings sensed that
Damian was a jewel among postmen.

One day, Damian failed to appear. On the third day,
several people noticed that they were no longer getting
letters, and on the fourth a new postman appeared—
an impersonal and objective young man. A man who
reserved his heart for his own personal use and didn't
carry it around in his mailbag. He did his duty, but he
wasn't a ray of sunshine. One only really understands
what the sun is when it has disappeared behind a cloud.
A whole district started to miss Damian Hell.

The explanation was soon discovered and never understood. Damian was a bachelor. His postal round was
like a wife to him. One day there must have been a crisis
between them, he must have yearned for something new,
and he fell in love with a nice new suburb at the opposite

---

* *Hell* is German for light or bright

end of the city. For three days he traveled out to the new suburb and dropped letters at random in various boxes. Perhaps he was just bored with the old routine and tried in his fashion to introduce a little variety into his life. My explanations carry no medical authority. The psychiatrists into whose care Damian was placed will have been able to come up with a more scientific account. Before long, he was dismissed as posing no threat to the public and now draws a small pension, works as a handyman, and sings. The mailman has been forgotten, while as a handyman he has some pale shadow of his erstwhile popularity.

Johanna has often been a faithless lover and always a faithful friend. While others shrugged their shoulders and declared that Damian was mad, she gave blazing defenses of his actions as a display of normality. Only a madman or an idiot, she declared, was capable of doing the same thing every day for decades. Damian's soul stood in need of something like its dirty weekend. In his mild, peaceable manner, he had given in to the lure of danger and adventure and uncertain outcome and muted it to a harmless joke. Other men, drawn by the lure of the uncanny (the *Unheimlich* in Freud) into the practice of strangeness would have turned straightforwardly to evil—would have become murderers, vandals, torturers, arsonists, child molesters, swindlers, racketeers, or some other wickedness.

It may be observed that the multiplicity of evildoing demands a far greater vocabulary than goodness, which is rooted in singleness.

So, Johanna took care of Damian. Maybe she's right, and he is normal. He is a person who will never turn to the bad, either through his own agency or others'. Perhaps that's what matters. Johanna dragged me into a corner of the room with the cushions. Damian is singing. Johanna beams and applauds. In the opposite corner Anton is hunkering and muttering. "He's starting to get on my nerves," says Johanna, and waves and smiles at Anton. "I've had enough of him, Ferdinand—but maybe I love him still, I don't know. Of course, I've spoiled him by being too nice to him. But if I like someone, I want to be nice to them, I don't want to watch myself the whole time. I don't want to resort to those tricks that women use in order to keep a man." Johanna tells me she likes to be sweet and good to a man, then she gets up and gives the scowling Anton a medium-strength slap in the face.

While Anton takes himself off silently and with impressive dignity, Damian sings, "My friends, life is worth living..."

"If he's not back in an hour, will you go and get him for me?" says Johanna, and sashays out into the courtyard.

Johanna is wearing an off-the-shoulder red silk dress with a scary décolletage. Aloisia is wearing much the same thing. I don't understand what keeps such dresses from slipping. It looks very nice, but I'm sorry for the poor ladies who are prevented by the dictates of fashion from running around in the altogether. Especially when they wear their sundresses, they sometimes make a positively wretched impression on me. When I see them, I get the feeling they are awake at all hours, racking their brains as to how the tiny strips of material round their hips and bosoms can be made still tinier.

Aloisia is drinking champagne, and she is so boisterously cheerful, it's as though there never was anything like a Hugo Moppe in her life. My sister Nina, who is a painter in Munich, is drawing caricatures on the walls. She arrived sometime this morning, I haven't had a chance to speak to her yet. She seems to have turned into a calm and serious-minded girl.

Laura and her retinue were supposed to have arrived this morning as well. She was to have been the focus of the party. Johanna loves Laura and had intended a queenly role for her. Probably she would now be lying on one of the sofas, sleeping blissfully through all the racket. Now it looks as though Laura won't get here till tomorrow, when the party's safely over. I won't go home, I'll go straight to the station.

My brother Toni is here. He's sitting in a corner, looking as though he's about to cry. He came up from Starnberg yesterday. I had trouble recognizing him. The cheerful lad, the sunny boy of the family, he isn't cheerful anymore. Destiny has struck him a hard blow.

Poor Toni has become a little remote to me. When he was far away in the South, we were closer.

Starnberg is where he has his nursery. He won't have been coining it exactly, and will have had the usual economic anxieties as per. He didn't care, though. All those things he wasn't able to afford didn't matter to him. He was happy with his little Mariechen and their pets. At least he thought he was. A couple of weeks ago, an acquaintance gave him a mild case of lottery fever. The first three times he didn't win, and he was all set to give up. But then he tried it a fourth time. Mariechen posted his entry. She conscientiously gave the receipt to her husband. Shortly after, Toni saw that he had won 48,000 marks. There was no doubt about it, he had won. He went crazy. First slightly crazy, then completely crazy. He bought clothes for Mariechen in which she looks like a bedraggled film star who's been in a bicycle accident. He bought all sorts of stuff for the house and the yard and the nursery. He played host to all their friends. Probably he bought his bees a jeroboam of champagne. He wanted to spend a day of his life being foolish. Then he started making plans—new buildings, new nursery extensions, new stables. He became obsessed with breeding orchids. He wanted to keep monkeys, order tulips from Holland, retile the bathroom, and lots more. There's no end of great and small wishes that a person can collect in the course of a lifetime.

And then came the catastrophe. Toni had indeed won, but the money wasn't paid out to him and presumably never will be. Registered mail rarely gets lost, but Toni's registered letter was. The lottery panel refused to shell out, and the post only pays its standard forty marks for a lost registered letter. Toni doesn't understand, he can't let the matter rest, he thinks the post is obliged to indemnify him, he wants to go to court. If the unhappy man had seen he had made a mistake, he would probably have settled down sooner or later. But as it is, he continues to hope and is getting more and more deranged. If he tells people now what he wants to do with the money, you get the sense that even a million wouldn't be enough. He tells everyone about his mishap, it's all the conversation he has. He asks everyone for advice, and everyone advises him differently. This afternoon I saw him standing with a small boy in front of an ice cream van, and I'm sure he was talking about the criminal deceit of the postal service. If you try telling him to be sensible, he looks at you as if he'd suddenly noticed he was with his mortal enemy. Mariechen is running around looking tearstained and puffy-faced and has already consulted Aloisia about the advisability of a divorce. I think Toni wouldn't mind. He could then devote himself entirely to his lottery win.

Just now he's hunkered in a corner looking to see whom he could discuss the post's skulduggery with. It looks as though everyone has already heard the story, and no one wants to hear it a second time.

Just now I see Herr Pittermann sitting down beside Toni. Pittermann looks flushed and a little woozy, but is evidently trying to compose his carnivalesque face. Pittermann is just the right person, Pittermann will cluck like a mother hen and turn a little profit on the side.

Pittermann used to be a rep for a toy company. He was always a jovial, life-affirming character, a doughty carnival supporter, indispensable at weddings, funerals, baptisms, and other celebrations. He loves the songs of the Rhineland, Rhine wine, and Rhine jokes. His life, though, has repeatedly brought him into unhappy situations, in which he managed to prevail through bravery, resourcefulness, and optimism. Johanna met him through a businesswoman for whom he promised to organize a telephone. Telephone connections are still not easily come by. Pittermann has promised Johanna a telephone as well.

Pittermann can get hold of just about anything, he has connections, which is to say human connections. Or so he claims. Of course, the connections cost money. Or they demand payment in kind. For instance, the businesswoman passed on a whole lot of sardines and cognac. The connections love cognac. They smoke as well. Pittermann does it all for nothing. That way he is sometimes even more expensive than the connections by themselves. You have to show gratitude to him, have him round and spoil him. It's like with girls who give themselves to a man out of sheer love and won't accept any presents. You end up having to take them to expensive restaurants and bars, put them in cabs, and send them flowers and perfumes and boxes of chocolates. For all that, a man could easily get himself a month with a girl he could pay. But there's no sense in trying to explain things like that to my mother-in-law or Meta Kolbe, they just get angry.

Pittermann has promises of telephones outstanding to another ten people. Or maybe more than that by now. At any rate, ten people have now got together to form an anti-Pittermann trust. Pittermann's connection has let him down. The suspicion has surfaced that he himself may be the connection. Anyway, to date no one has a telephone, and dark clouds are gathering over Pittermann's head.

Before the currency reform Pittermann had a very lucrative and rather more innocuous idea. Again using his connections, he engaged himself on behalf of people who wanted or needed to be de-Nazified. They were innocuous cases, but it was precisely these innocuous cases that were nervous and anxious. Pittermann propped them up, Pittermann lent them support. One day they were de-Nazified. They would have been without Pittermann's intervention. Whereas Pittermann would probably have perished of hunger and thirst long before the currency reform without the de-Nazification scheme.

I wonder what possibilities the Pittermannesque brain would see in a situation like Toni's. I can see the wheels turning, and Toni is looking optimistic, almost happy.

Soon it'll be tomorrow. Noise and drink chew up the time, the hours turn into minutes. And vice versa.

Anton is back. He is sitting with Johanna and a policeman who has come to see about the noise. Johanna welcomed the policeman with delight, he was one she knew from another life. I'd like to meet someone Johanna hasn't known in another life. The policeman is singing and having a high old time.

In the lending library reconfigured as a bar, Mother Peipel's curtains have fallen victim to the flames. A few books are lying in puddles on the floor. Heinrich and Magnesius distinguished themselves as first responders. I have a singed eyebrow and a hole in my trousers. I don't usually like catastrophes, but there was something refreshing about this one. Rowdy parties are much of a muchness, and a little interruption seemed to me very much called for. I don't like to sing, and I prefer to do my drinking and kissing in private.

Luitpold and his wife Lucca are wandering across
the courtyard arm in arm, sweeping glasses off the table.
"I'm surprised at you, burying yourself in your middle-
class business," I said to him, "you take everything so
seriously, even when we barely know what will happen tomorrow, and we're just living from day-to-day."
Luitpold didn't reply, and Lucca looked startled. "Since
when do you talk such nonsense, Ferdinand?" she said,
"Ever since there have been human beings on the planet
they've lived from day-to-day and have no idea if they'll
be gravely ill tomorrow or suffer a calamity the day after.
You act as though war was the only calamity in the world,
but there are floods and tornadoes and volcanoes and
earthquakes—people have lived from day-to-day for
thousands of years."

"She's right," said Luitpold. Lucca is always right.

Heinrich is lying in Meta Kolbe's embrace. He will
regret it tomorrow.

Luise, my fiancée, is dancing, I don't know her part-
ner. Gradually my eyes are swimming. Luise seems wor-
ried to me, I have probably neglected her. Luitpold is so
happy with Lucca. I wonder if I could ever be as happy as
he is? I don't know. At the moment I'd be hard-pressed
to say what happiness is, and whether I even want to be
happy. But I don't want Luise to suffer. "Come on, Luise,
let's drink a bottle of champagne together—here in the
courtyard, at the far end of the table, we can have a little

privacy." Luise sets off after me, her expression is sad.
I pop open a bottle of champagne. Will I ever have the
courage to tell her the truth? The sky is just beginning
to brighten, the paper lanterns have gone out. At the
opposite end of the table, Damian the singing postman
is asleep with his head on the table like a traveler in a
third-class waiting-room who's missed his connection.

Luise's hair looks colorless and scruffy, she is in an
ugly turquoise dress. She is wearing a triple strand of
wax pearls and a broach on her bosom in the form of a
spider with brass legs and a shimmering pebble for a
belly. She looks so cheap and wretched that I am almost
moved. Her posture is awful. She is sitting there with
her chin in her hands. I'm just wondering what to say
to her when I notice that she's crying. Oh, what now?
I feel an upsurge of detestable feelings. I'd like to run
away and leave her all alone, I'd like to smack her face;
I want to say I've had enough and have had for as long
as I can remember. And all the time I feel sorry for her,
and think I'm being mean. I fill our glasses, say "There,
there, what's the matter?" and light a cigarette. I give her
shoulder a little shake. Luise's quiet crying turns into an
audible sob. It's terrible not being able to comfort crying
women. As soon as they have your pity, they can't stop.
With positively sadistic pleasure, they kneel down in
their puddle of misery. I feel like saying "Go on, have a
drink!" but feel that every word I could utter would only

be more barbarous. It's getting chill, and Luise is cold. She has goosebumps on her arms. Crying as she is, I really don't want to drag her indoors.

"All right, let's drink," Luise suddenly says, with a little quaver in her voice. We do so. We do so again. Luise has a big gulp. And then she starts to speak: "Well, it had to happen, Ferdinand, I'm very fond of you, I really am, otherwise I'd have told you long ago. But with you always fixing everything about the house, and mother saying you're a useful fellow to have around. You remember, before the currency reform, when money wasn't worth anything, and you couldn't get anyone to work for you, unless you offered them an arm and a leg. And we didn't have anything to eat either, and you kept producing stuff out of thin air, but that's not really it—"

I'm not really following at this stage, presumably Luise is drunk. I don't care if she is, nothing'll happen to her here. So long as she stops crying. I pour us some more. "Cheers, Luise."

Luise's stout little hand clasps the narrow stem of the champagne glass. "Go on, drink, then you can go on."

"Well, please understand, Ferdi, and please don't take it amiss. See, Papa's de-Nazified now, and he can get a proper job, and other men are earning as well. Of course, everything's terribly expensive, but we're able to buy vegetables and get our shoes resoled. I know it was really nice of you to repair our shoes, but a proper shoemaker does it better. Mama says you never had a proper training in it. Papa says, he's perfectly fine about you, but you were a man for abnormal times. And now the times are getting much more normal, or don't you find? We spent so long walking around bareheaded, but Mama and I are getting three hats made, each. You can't really walk around without a hat anymore, and that's an indication, don't you think, about the times getting to be more normal?"

"So, I'm not a man for normal times, Luise?"

"No, Ferdi, you're really not. I mean, when people are wearing hats again, and not those headscarves, and you never want to go for a nice promenade on Sundays either. I hardly know what to say when someone asks, What does your fiancé do? I always say, Oh, he's an academic. But you're not really an academic, are you?"

"No, I'm not. Why should I be an academic? I never claimed to be an academic. Have some more, Luise?"

"Thanks, Ferdi, here's looking at you. I really have nothing against you. Don't think I'm being silly—there's no law that says a man has to be an academic, and I know academics these days earn a pittance, and other men provide a much more solid basis. But you're not a businessman either, or a civil servant. Don't think I'm uncouth, I appreciate artists too. They can be very decent people, with a regular income and everything. But you're not an artist either. I'm not saying you're not a regular person, but you're not really anything, are you. I'm sure you're not a bad man, we always thought the world of you, because you were so well brought up and a bit shy and never expected anything. Papa once wanted to tell you that you did a really bad job with the guttering, but Mama and I wouldn't have it because we felt so sorry for you. It turned into a proper scene, and you once told me I never put up any fight."

I don't remember ever having said anything like that to Luise. My head is buzzing. Damian has gone to sleep and is snoring; his snoring is pleasanter to listen to than his singing.

"Of course you can put up a fight, Luise," I say.

"Well, I want to wish you all the best in your life to come," says Luise, "you know, I once thought of writing to you, but then I didn't. I really didn't like you at first, but then I didn't want to be that way, and you were a soldier, fighting for the Fatherland. And then I was a soldier's girl, and I had to wait for you to come home, because that was my duty. And then you were coming out of POW camp and it wasn't right to disappoint a homecomer. You have no idea what scornful looks I got from all the other girls. And then you went and made yourself useful and you did odd jobs about the house, and only a man who's head over heels in love would do that. Please now, Ferdinand, promise you won't kill yourself and don't hurt me just because

I can't respond to your love. I've said it now—now that times are normal again."

I promised Luise that I wouldn't kill myself over her, and that I wouldn't hurt her either. I feel incredibly stupid. For long tormenting years I've been wanting to be rid of Luise, and now I learn that I never had her anyway. "Well, cheers, Luise—bottoms up."

The dawn breeze blows masonry dust from the rubble into my eyes. I feel like whooping for joy, but I can't. All these difficulties and awkwardnesses had become cornerstones of my existence. Against my will, I had committed myself to Luise and her family. The commitment has ended, and instead of feeling happy about it, I feel discombobulated. It must be the way a criminal feels after spending years trying to avoid the consequences of an action, when a sudden miracle slips him free of guilt and conscience. In this instant, I can understand my landlady Frau Stabhorn, who suffered for years from an ingrown toenail on her left foot and felt bereft when an orthopedic surgeon cut it out. No normal human being loves pain, no normal person loves his pain and gets used to his pain. But there comes to be an intimacy with it, he respects it, he treats it better than he treats anything else in this world, he is afraid of it, and hates it and fights it. And not until he's rid of it does he understand how strong the symbiosis was. He's freed but not yet relieved. He experiences a temporary disorientation.

"I don't understand," said Luise, as I tried to explain my nebulous thoughts to her, "but I'm pleased everything's all right now—you know, we had this really crazy carpenter once, he talked a bit like you, but he was very good at his job as well, and that's where you're different."

I kiss Luise's hand and promise never to forget her. No, I'm not so dull that I can't feel a little intimation of liberty. "Be sure something becomes of you, Ferdinand," says a lurching Luise as I lead her back inside, "be sure something becomes of you, if only for my sake."

I hand over Luise to an indistinct tangle of humanity. She pushes on in the direction of a male figure—I think it is the man she was dancing with before. "An engineer at Ford," says Johanna, "after the war he was something in the Planning Ministry and made a fortune with black-market plaster. A player. Nothing happened to him because he had protection." I ask Johanna if he's a man for normal times. "These aren't normal times," says Johanna, "but I knew him long ago, he got hold of some tiles for me and diddled me."

"Here, Ferdinand," calls my brother Toni, "this is my friend Pittermann—he's going to help me out. Pittermann is my friend. You're my friend, aren't you, Pittermann? Pittermann has connections in the post office and knows some pretty high-up people." For now, Pittermann is finishing a Carnival song, and when he's done, he tells me he means to find interested parties

who will pay five marks to represent Toni's interests.
Each of them stands to earn three hundred marks for his
original outlay, once Toni collects his 48,000 winnings.
"It's just the way I am," says Pittermann, "I try to help
people, I don't feel at ease with myself if I'm not helping
someone—basically I have no interest in these sorts of
things, one only ever encounters ingratitude, I'm pres-
ently representing a rainwater enterprise—but you won't
understand. By the way, did you hear the one about the
woman who raised her left leg?"

"Why, there you are, Comrade," comes a bellow
behind me, "do you remember Sergeant Stolpe, and
whatever happened to Fennkopf?" I have no idea. I see
an ill-shaven man with skew tie, stubbly reddish hair,
and little light-blue eyes. It's Robert Leberfeld, my old
comrade and savior. He's been in Cologne for a week
now. For a week now, he's been glued to my tracks like
some master detective.

During the war, Leberfeld was a sergeant of mine.
He wasn't awful, but he didn't arouse any particular
enthusiasm in me either. There was no personal re-
lationship between us till the day Leberfeld saved my
life. During an unexpected artillery barrage I had taken
cover, busted my ankle, and couldn't get up. Leberfeld
came running back, hoicked me up, and panting carried
me two miles to the field dispensary, even though I was
just about capable of hobbling.

I was moved and grateful, and from then on Leberfeld looked after me the way an animal lover might adopt
a pathetic stray. He viewed me as belonging to him, and
he is one of those people who look after their property.
I had to sit with Leberfeld in the evening, and he would
tell me jokes, the stupidest and nastiest jokes I've ever
heard in my life. His supply of these was apparently
inexhaustible—or at least it hadn't been exhausted by the
time we parted at the end of six months. When he wasn't
telling jokes, Leberfeld liked to talk about women and
brothels and sexual experiences, his own and others'. I
can't imagine how anyone after three weeks of Leberfeld would have any interest in a love affair. Mine was
certainly gone, and for the foreseeable future. Of course,
I listened to Leberfeld. What else was I to do? He was my
sergeant, and on top of that he had saved my life. It upset
me to feel hatred welling up in me against my rescuer,
and I did all I could to fight it down. I would much rather
Bernard Shaw had saved my life. I missed out on such
a lot. I had to be grateful to have been rescued at all, I
suppose, even if it was Leberfeld. But the man made it
difficult for me to esteem him as I ought.

A week ago, Leberfeld showed up. I hadn't seen him
in years. "Don't you remember me then, old codger?"
Yes, I did. I asked him to supper. I was happy to be able to
take him out and so do something for him. But Leberfeld
didn't need my help, in fact he wanted to pay for me. He's

taken over a transport company in a Cologne suburb, and he's doing very well. He has so little in the way of practical worries that he can afford to seek out emotional contacts. Finding me—his old comrade whose life he saved—causes him to shed tears of happiness. "Jesus, fellow, now we'll paint the town together—eh what? I expect you know your way around here. At least a fellow can talk to you. Do you still remember what fantastic conversations we used to have? Remind me to tell you a couple of jokes—I bet you won't have heard these before— you'll piss yourself laughing—at least with you, a man knows he's not casting swine before pearls. Christ, we'll have so much to talk about!" And so I pushed off with my rescuer. I spent three evenings and half the ensuing nights with him. I got rid of Luise tonight, but I'll never get rid of Leberfeld. He's all right, but really I can't stand him. If any and all soldiers weren't appalling to me, I could take it into my head to join the Foreign Legion. I'm hoping it'll be enough if I just leave Cologne.

Then again, I might find myself missing Leber-feld's joviality. His cluelessness as to my real feelings is beginning to charm me. Also, I won't find it easy to give up my volunteer work for Luise and her parents. People's claims on me tether me to life. I will be pleased to go on being useful to Luise every so often.

Johanna's rooms are starting to empty out. The guests are leaving like ghosts struck by the dawn light.

Just a moment ago they were here, now they're suddenly gone. It seems to me they vanished into thin air. I can see my brother Toni totter off with Pittermann. The fool has let himself be talked out of his simple, uncomplaining existence; I must have a word with him tomorrow.

"Now," says Johanna, "that was a nice party, wasn't it? Not a lot happened, but all the glasses are broken. Anyone who's still here and wants a drink will have to drink out of the bottle." Johanna's guests have left an unholy mess. She's looking at a mega clearing-up session. She won't be able to open her library till the day after tomorrow.

"Put up a sign, Johanna: 'Closed for renovation.'"

The now-broken glasses had been borrowed, and Johanna will have to replace them. Who's going to pay for them? Johanna hasn't any money. We should pass the hat around. Johanna laughs at the suggestion.

"You can get money out of people before a party, Ferdinand, and during a party, but never afterwards, you surely ought to know that."

Well: people who have exhausted themselves while celebrating often turn into misers in the subsequent period of sobering up. Johanna sits up on her counter, the dawn stains her red dress red.

She says: "I'm wondering if I should start tidying up now, or just go to sleep in this godawful pigsty. Wouldn't it be nice to have a tidy room left over with a tidy bed

in it? But I don't have either one. You know what I wish
I had, Ferdinand? A proper separate bedroom with a
separate bed in it. I can't stand this combination of
bedsit-kitchen anymore. And I hate convertible couches,
they're neither one thing nor another."

Johanna pulls open the door of her store. She looks
dreamily out into the distance.

"Look at that, Ferdinand—see the sky on fire! It's the
sunrise. In an hour's time the first bailiff will be here."

Awake with tiredness, I wander off to the station.
It's a clear, bright morning. The ruins are in bloom.
New houses and little shops springing up among them.
A beggar weaves past a colorful fruit stand and begins
singing. "Do people give each other roses in Tirol . . ."
Industrious fellow, starting his day so early. He is old
but well preserved and has a beautiful drinker's nose.
I give him a mark and hope he buys himself a nice
brandy with it.

"I'll walk with you a bit, you seem to have forgotten
me," says a voice at my side. It's Lenchen. I really had
forgotten her. Her features are still and tired and her
walk a little sluggish. But her forehead, eyes, and smile
are still friendly and fresh. I link arms with her and lead
her on, that way she can have a little frail presleep. It
makes me glad to know I can help this creature. There is
an obstacle in her path, and just at the moment she is too
weak to jump it all by herself. Someone has to lend her

a hand, then she can do it. And she won't cling on to me once she's able to walk on unassisted.

I drop Lenchen off at pretty Fräulein Kuckuck's. I have time to drink a cup of coffee there on my feet.

"I don't think there's ever been a person who was always able to fend for themselves, not since the beginning of the world," I say, once I've burned my mouth on the hot coffee, "and I don't think there's ever been a person who wasn't helped by others either. The shame of it is that it was almost always too late, or insufficient or the wrong kind of help."

"Drink up," says Fräulein Kuckuck, "Lenchen needs to go to bed, and I wouldn't mind another hour's sleep myself, so why don't you hold the rest of your morning service on your way to the station. What is it with men, that they like to wax philosophical when they've had a few? They can't find an end, and ideally they would start crying at their own nobility. Finish your coffee and get lost—hang on, I'll give your hair a quick comb, and brush the ash off your collar. You can clean your fingernails yourself. You won't want your mother to see you looking like that, will you?"

I was pressed down onto a chair and felt like an old stove being violently scrubbed and brought to a shine. Lenchen too perked up a little and was seized by the sadistic feminine desire to grab a helpless object and work on it with chemicals and vicious implements towards its ostensible cleansing. I think in the hurry of the moment, I was even vacuumed, and rubbed with washing powder and sprinkled with Vim. As a finishing touch, Lenchen wiped my nose and Fräulein Kuckuck pushed three particularly thorny roses into my hand.

I stood on the platform, lonely as a crumb. The train had pulled in, but no Laura got out. With heavy feet I tramped back down the malicious station steps.

Rooms had been booked for Laura at a nearby hotel. I went there, thinking maybe the porter had been given a message. The roses drooped in my sweating hand.

"Yes, sir," said the porter, "the party arrived on the evening train."

I walked up the stairs, feeling the sweet softness of a stair carpet. I gave a quiet tap on the door and turned the handle. The door was open. Laura doesn't like to lock doors. That unlocked door was the first intimation of home.

At the foot of a large bed was a narrow sofa with a little dachshund sitting on it, viewing me gravely.

I didn't move. I heard some calm breathing, and I knew I was in the right room. The curtains were drawn tight, and the light in the room was compounded from pink corals and old silver.

I looked at the bed. Four gobstopper eyes were looking at me. They belonged to two little black children with black woolly heads. These earnest little joke items observed me silently, alert and awake. And with that regal superiority and calm that only the consciousness of deep security is capable of imparting.

Between them Laura lay sleeping. Her hair shone darkly, and her face had the familiar calm beauty. I felt ashamed of my momentary apprehension.

I sat down next to the well-bred little dachshund and said to myself, Let's not wake her. Once more I had the happy if fleeting sense that I'd come home.

IRMGARD KEUN was born in Berlin in
1905. She published her first novel, *Gilgi, One
of Us*, in 1931. Her second novel, *The Artificial
Silk Girl*, became an instant bestseller in
1932, but was then blacklisted by the Nazis.
Eventually sentenced to death, she fled the
country and staged her own suicide before
sneaking back into Germany, where she
lived undercover for the duration of the war.
She later resumed writing under the name
of Charlotte Tralow, enjoying only modest
success until her early works were rediscov-
ered and reissued in the late 1970s. She died
in Cologne in 1982.

MICHAEL HOFMANN has translated the
work of Gottfried Benn, Hans Fallada,
Franz Kafka, Joseph Roth, and many others.
In 2012 he was awarded the Thornton Wilder
Prize for Translation by the American
Academy of Arts and Letters. His *Selected
Poems* was published in 2009, *Where Have You
Been? Selected Essays* in 2014, and *One Lark,
One Horse: Poems* in 2019. He lives in Florida
and London.